BLUE MOONLIGHTING

Detective Bobby Simone told himself he wasn't on duty now. His NYPD day shift was over and he was moonlighting as a security guard.

A special kind of guard for a special kind of security.

Manhattan mogul Michael Wynn was paying Bobby a pile to keep daughter Laura off the sauce and on the straight and narrow.

Trouble was, Wynn hadn't provided Bobby with anyone to guard him. There was no one to stop her from kissing him. Deeply. Her tongue probing, gently, then thrusting, until he caught her up in his arms and they fell onto the soft bed, his hands sliding up onto her breasts.

"Gimme a second," she murmured. She slipped off the bed and pulled the black turtleneck over her head, revealing a cotton camisole, and her breasts were so full they didn't flatten out when she slipped the flimsy underthing over her head. Then she unzipped her jeans and Bobby thought, *This is wrong, so wrong. . . .*

He was right about that.

NYPD BLUE:™
BLUE BLOOD

a novel by
Max Allan Collins

Based on the television series
created by David Milch & Steven Bochco

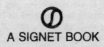

A SIGNET BOOK

SIGNET
Published by the Penguin Group
Penguin Putnam Inc., 375 Hudson Street,
New York, New York 10014, U.S.A.
Penguin Books Ltd, 27 Wrights Lane,
London W8 5TZ, England
Penguin Books Australia Ltd, Ringwood,
Victoria, Australia
Penguin Books Canada Ltd, 10 Alcorn Avenue,
Toronto, Ontario, Canada M4V 3B2
Penguin Books (N.Z.) Ltd, 182–190 Wairau Road,
Auckland 10, New Zealand

Penguin Books Ltd, Registered Offices:
Harmondsworth, Middlesex, England

First published by Signet, an imprint of Dutton Signet,
a member of Penguin Putnam Inc.

First Printing, September, 1997
10 9 8 7 6 5 4 3 2 1

PUBLISHER'S NOTE
This is a work of fiction. Names, characters, places, and incidents either
are the product of the author's imagination or are used fictitiously,
and any resemblance to actual persons, living or dead, events, or locales
is entirely coincidental.

For Matthew Clemens—
true-blue friend

Author's Note

This book is not a "novelization" of episodes of *NYPD Blue*, but an original story based on that award-winning series.

Steven Bochco and David Milch (and their various gifted collaborators) have created an ongoing novel on film, and I have attempted to remain true to their characters and continuity. This story is an "episode" that takes place between the second and third seasons of the series, relatively early in the relationship between Detectives Andy Sipowicz and Bobby Simone.

I would like to acknowledge the following books: *True Blue* (1995), David Milch and Det. Bill Clark; *Infamous Manhattan* (1996), Andrew Roth; *The Detectives* (1994), Peter A. Michaels; and *Cop Talk* (1994), E. W. Count. Also, *NYPD Blue* FAQ (http://www.crpht.lu/FAQ/tv/nypd-blue/nypd-blue.html) compiled by Alan Sepinwall. Thanks to Pamela Cecil, Michael Cornelison, and Robert J. Randisi for answering research questions; my wife, Barbara Collins, for assistance and research help; and editor Danielle Perez for her patience.

—M.A.C.

"Every detective has strengths and weaknesses"

—Detective Bill Clark

ONE

Detective Andy Sipowicz, 15th Precinct, 47 years of age, 17 years on the job, eight months sober, was two months married.

He would have been sober longer, and married longer, but last year he'd inadvertently fallen off the wagon when he'd given in to a drink at a social occasion. Not just any social occasion, either: a party with Sylvia's family, Greeks, and they like to dance and they like to touch and they like to drink. Sipowicz wasn't big on the first two, but had way too much experience with the third.

And, so, Sylvia had been exposed to Andy Sipowicz at his worst. What a lovely, intelligent woman like Sylvia Costas wanted to do with a homely hump like him, at his best, was something Sipowicz never understood. Sober, he was no prize, two-hundred-and-too-many pounds of balding protoplasm with dark-circled eyes and skimpy mustache which he would have shaved off, only without it his round lumpy puss would have had no color at all.

Sylvia was this nicely rounded female creature with soft brown hair and softer brown eyes and creamy complexion, and she had a better job than he did, too. Assistant D.A.s made twice what second grade detectives did, and maybe that was why he had called her a pissy little bitch that time, on the courthouse steps.

He would have liked to think he wasn't himself when he said that to her; he'd been half in the bag (drinking on the job was actually rare for him, but he had justified it as needed help for the court appearance) and overanxious to nail that scungill asshole Alfonse Giardella. He'd come off real bad on the stand and A.D.A. Costas had been no help, even blaming him for it, after. Looking back, he knew she was right; but at the time, he had felt persecuted, and got ugly with her.

Like most drunks, Sipowicz's greatest fear was that the real him was exactly who Sylvia had seen that time on the courthouse steps, and that worse time when her well-meaning Greek kinfolks included him in a toast that sent him cartwheeling off the wagon.

She had seen the mean, abusive bastard that alcohol unleashed and she still loved him. Loved him anyway, and he had climbed back on the wagon, and two months ago, in a big church in a fancy-ass ceremony in front of more cops and Greeks than a precinct house in Athens, and the grown son who had also forgiven him for being him, this beautiful smart woman had married this ugly dumb man.

They were a married couple now, unbelievable but true, and he'd abandoned his shabby second-floor walk-up on East Seventh for her cozy second-floor apartment in Gramercy Park, adjusting to a habitat of ferns and dried flowers and Victorian touches.

She had granted him a position of prominence for his treasured tropical fish tank, just inside the door, in a living room otherwise dominated by ornately framed wall hangings, tasteful pastel furnishings, and filmy swag curtains. Though he'd halfway moved in prior to the wedding (but holding on to his own hole-in-the-wall till the vows were taken) there were few signs that Andy Sipowicz lived here. The kitchenette, off the living room, had a bulletin board with "funny" feminist cartoons and family photos and food-oriented wall hangings, though nothing too obnoxious.

The bedroom, however, with its antique wardrobe and radiator lined with hardcover books, was strictly Sylvia's domain, frilly framed pictures of flowers and dead relatives on walls painted a soothing pink. (Wasn't that the color the shrinks said induced suicide?)

This afternoon, a Sunday, he had enlisted his partner, Bobby Simone, to help him carry up the stairs, in various pieces, the latest addition to the Sylvia Costas collection: the fancy black wrought-iron bed she had spotted in a SoHo shop.

"What are you gonna do with *your* old stuff?" Bobby had asked him, halfway up the first flight.

"The Salvation Army and Good Will are in a bidding war," Sipowicz had said. His furniture was in temporary storage in the basement of his old building.

"Seriously," Bobby said, chewing gum, breathing

easily. The tall, dark, good-looking detective maintained his easy grace even while shlepping a cumbersome headboard up a narrow flight of stairs. "I got a cousin could use a few things. College kid sleeping on his apartment floor."

"Hey, take it all," Sipowicz panted. "Before some museum grabs it as a specimen of urban blight."

Now, the married couple that the Sipowiczes had become were repaying Andy's friend and partner with dinner. They were entertaining. Sylvia had served a Greek salad and leg of lamb with fluffy rice and all the trimmings (her father was in the restaurant business), and now their guest was on the couch, leaning back happily stuffed, while Mrs. Sipowicz fussed with coffee and baklava squares in the kitchenette. The window-mounted air-conditioner was thrumming.

It was September but summer hadn't quite turned into fall, yet. The two men still wore the sport shirts and jeans they'd hauled the bed up in; Sylvia wore a summery blue-and-white flower print dress. Sipowicz, sprawled in his well-worn easy chair, one of the few items imported from his former ignoble bachelor quarters, smiled to himself, thinking, *Ozzie and freakin' Harriet.*

The couch was a little low for Bobby, and his long legs were akimbo. "And she can cook," he said, with a contented sigh and a lift of the eyebrows.

Sipowicz grunted. "Yeah, I'm really missin' my wild bachelor days. Them Hungry Man dinners, I could microwave the hell out of them."

Bobby's smile was typically shy. "You did good, Andy."

"Second time's a charm," he said, in reference to his disastrous first marriage. Then he shrugged. "Life could be better. I could hit the Lotto."

"Sylvia's got a nice eye for decorating." Bobby touched the quilt with the fish-pattern slung over the couch.

"John gave me that."

"John Kelly?"

Sipowicz shook his head no. "Upstairs John."

The ladylike quilt was a wedding gift from that gangly gay fill-in receptionist who "styled" Andy's remaining hair from time to time, Sipowicz battling his homophobia by accepting free hair cuts.

"What do you hear from the other John?"

"Sent us a card . . . a Hallmark."

Bobby seemed to think about that for a few moments, then said, "I know it disappointed you, him not making the wedding."

Sipowicz smirked. "He was in India, protectin' dotheads from a death cult."

It sounded like a joke, but Sipowicz's former partner—who'd left the department under a cloud—was doing full-time security, now.

Sipowicz shrugged. "You work with a guy every day for seven, eight years, you think you're tight. But maybe it's one of them superficial things. Maybe that's all these work 'friendships' are."

"Well, it meant a lot to me, Andy, you asking me to be your best man."

Embarrassed, Sipowicz said, "I didn't mean anything about us by that remark," but really he had.

Bobby sat forward, his hands folded between his long legs. "You know, Andy—I never met your partner, but I hear he was a stand-up guy."

Sipowicz shrugged again.

"What I hear, he didn't leave the job 'cause he wanted to." Bobby's eyes tightened. "Probably the only way he could handle it was make a clean break."

"Prob'ly."

Sylvia brought them coffee and baklava, but didn't join them, returning to the kitchen to wash dishes, turning down all offers of help.

"Quite a lady," Bobby said admiringly.

"They ain't makin' feminists like they used to." Sipowicz cleared his throat, sat up, and struggled for the words to get into a subject he'd been thinking of raising all night. "Listen, uh . . . if I'm out of line . . ."

"What, Andy?"

"Nothin'. Forget I mentioned it."

Bobby flashed a half smile. "You didn't mention anything, yet."

Bobby Simone was his partner, and Sipowicz had accepted him, but social occasions—and getting personal—were new to this relationship. Maybe thinking of John Kelly as a son, maybe taking Kelly into his goddamned heart, and then having Kelly disappear out of his life like a fart in the wind, was making Sipowicz gun-shy in his middle age.

"What is it, Andy?" Bobby seemed unsure of

whether to be amused or concerned by his partner's discomfort.

Finally Sipowicz spit it out: "You haven't been seein' anybody, have ya, lately? Of the female persuasion?"

Now Bobby was clearly amused, his smile a halfmoon above the coffee cup he had just sipped from. "Why? Does Sylvia have a sister?"

Sipowicz threw up his hands. "Hey! I'm out of line. Sorry."

"Don't be silly. Speak your mind."

"Well, you were seein' Russell, for a while there."

Bobby had been dating Detective Diane Russell, who had fairly recently transferred to the 15th Squad after a long undercover stint; but right around the time Andy and Sylvia got married, the relationship had abruptly ended.

Bobby's amusement faded. "Yeah. Yeah, I was, Andy."

Sipowicz avoided his partner's steady, almost accusing gaze. "Look, we both know you two was a pretty nice couple, had a nice thing goin'. But, hell— I understand why you broke it off."

"*She* broke it off, Andy."

"Oh. That I wasn't aware of."

"But she came back, if you're interested, and then I broke it off. . . . And you know why."

"Yeah, that's uh . . . why I brung it up."

Bobby's gaze was openly accusing, now. "You were the one who first noticed it, Andy."

"Yeah. Yeah, I know."

Russell, a thorough-going professional in her late

twenties, a lithely beautiful young woman with a crinkly smile, lively eyes, and a full head of reddish-brown curls, had something in common with Andy Sipowicz besides their line of work: she was an alcoholic.

"Drinkin' on the job, Andy," Bobby said, shaking his head, his expression one surprisingly void of compassion, "she coulda got somebody killed. Me or you, for example."

"That's a little extreme."

"I saw her pat down a skel and miss an ankle-holstered piece. That kind of get somebody killed."

"You haven't seen her, lately."

"No. You know she's on nights, now."

Sipowicz twitched a facial shrug. "Well, just don't be too hard on her, is all."

"I don't want anything to do with her," Bobby said firmly. "Not until, or unless, she gets her act together."

"Hey! Cut the kid some slack. She's got a home life right outta Jerry freakin' Springer. It takes a lotta spine to stand up and say you got a problem like she done."

"I didn't know you'd taken such an interest in her."

Sylvia, coming over with her own cup of coffee and baklava, smiled and said, "Neither did I."

Sipowicz said, "We was discussin' Detective Russell."

"I gathered." And she was smiling, but the way she might smile at a witness on the stand who she was about to eviscerate.

Sylvia sat on the couch beside their guest.

"It took me a long time to admit this," Sipowicz blurted, "but booze, for some of us . . . it's a sickness."

Sylvia softened and reached out and touched his nearest hand. "I know."

An awkward silence settled on the room.

"I'm not unsympathetic," Bobby said finally. "But this isn't something I can help her with."

"You're right," Sipowicz said. "You're exactly right. But if you happen to see her, run into her, whatever—a kind word wouldn't kill you."

Bobby nodded, smiled the shy smile. "Sorry. I guess I did sound like an asshole."

"Watch that," Sylvia said. "I won't have you infringing on my husband's territory."

"I think I been insulted," Sipowicz said, and got up and went into the kitchen to get himself another slab of baklava. "So, when do you start this security job?"

"I already have," Bobby said. "Timmons has got some kind of bodyguard gig lined up for me, starting tomorrow."

"I didn't know you were taking on night work," Sylvia said. "Why's a single guy like you need to drive himself so hard? Saving up for a sports car?"

Bobby twitched a humorless smile. "I still got doctors bills to pay. The insurance only covered about seventy percent, and we racked up a big tab."

Bobby's wife had died of cancer, a year and a half ago.

"Oh," Sylvia said, and her face fell. "I'm sorry. I didn't think . . ."

Bobby patted her hand. "That's okay. Really."

Sipowicz settled back into his chair, spoke through a mouthful of the confection. "Look, you need me to cover for you at work, just say the word."

"Thanks, Andy, but this shouldn't interfere with my regular eight to four."

Sylvia's eyes lit up. "You haven't seen our pictures!"

"No," Bobby said, while she got up and found the wedding album.

Sipowicz grinned at his partner. "And you thought dinner was gonna be free."

Much later, when his partner was gone, while he lay in the wrought-iron bed next to his wife, her back to him, in darkness relieved only by the glow of streetlights and neon edged along the window-shades, the bedroom's air-conditioner humming to the city's wailing siren and honking car horn tune, Andy Sipowicz touched Sylvia's shoulder. His rough fingers settled on creamy smoothness; she stirred, but he couldn't read whether the stirring was encouragement or dismissal—he wasn't that good a detective, and had not been married long enough to tell.

After all, they were newlyweds and still made love almost every night. But not tonight. Not yet, anyway.

"Some dinner," he said.

She murmured her thanks.

"I appreciate what you done tonight, uh . . . having Bobby over."

"I'm very tired."

"You, uh . . . don't wanna initiate this new bed or something?"

"I'm tired, Andy."

Her voice wasn't crabby or anything, so he kept at it.

"It was decent of Bobby, helpin' us out like that."

"Yes it was."

"He's a good kid."

"Yes he is."

"He liked your decorating and all."

"That's nice."

This was going nowhere, so he cuddled up to her, up to the smoothness of her silk nightgown, assuming the two-spoons position, close enough for her to know what he had in mind.

"Andy," she said crossly, as if to a child. "Not now."

Her tone irritated him. He pulled away from her. "So, what? The honeymoon's over, I take it."

She sat up in bed, turned to look at him, her face long with anger, her breasts round with what he wanted and wasn't going to get, tonight. "Andy, I'm tired. I cooked a very big meal, cleaned up with no help whatsoever from you—"

"Hey, I offered—"

"—and I'm in no mood, tonight. Do you understand?"

She lay on her back now, staring at the ceiling, arms folded tight, flattening those lovely breasts, and—detective that he was—he finally deduced that she was well and truly annoyed with him. He didn't think it had to do with cooking a meal or doing the dishes, either.

"What is it, Sylvia?" And with no sarcasm whatever, he asked, "What thoughtless thing have I done?"

"Nothing," she said.

He had interrogated enough perps to know a lie when he heard one.

"Come on, baby," he said, and gently, tentatively, he stroked her arm. "What?"

"I had ruled it out," she said, as if that were an answer.

"Ruled what out?"

Her lower lip trembled, but her lovely face was otherwise stone. "I had assumed it was nothing to worry about. That I could think the best of you."

"What?"

"Friday, I stopped by the stationhouse, to surprise you for lunch. But you were gone."

"Friday," he said, honestly not remembering. It was a whole day ago, after all. "What was Friday?"

She flashed him an accusatory look. "Bobby said you were probably at Rokka's."

The greasy little coffee shop was a cop hangout, near the precinct, and he'd had more meals there than he cared to remember.

And now it came to him: he'd had lunch with Russell.

"Yeah, I think that, uh . . . I did have lunch there yesterday."

"I know you did. I was going to join you till I

looked in the window and saw you already had a luncheon partner."

This would teach him, marrying a damn attorney.

"She's a fellow officer, Sylvia. We had lunch together. Hell, how many lunches have you had with Maury freakin' Abrams?"

"He's my boss." She was staring at the ceiling again. "Now this evening, I hear how interested you are in Detective Russell. How concerned for her welfare." And now her gaze turned on him, wounded puppy-dog eyes in a face clenched tight with accusation. "What's it about, Andy?"

Rage rose in him like a red rash. "Hey, I got the two-month itch, I guess. Did you follow us over to the Hotel Astor, where she had her legs in the air for me, all friggin' afternoon?"

Sylvia covered her mouth. "Oh, Andy."

Her eyes were tearing up. She was a strong woman, but even sober, he could summon words ugly enough to bring her to tears. Alcoholics are alcoholics even when they're dry.

"Christ, I'm sorry, baby," he said, reaching out for her.

"I'm *tired!*" she said, and turned her back to him, and pulled the sheet up over herself.

The argument—the first real argument of their marriage—was clearly over.

He turned his back to her, tried to sleep, but nothing came of it; he considered re-opening the discussion, and was about to offer an apology (even if he wasn't sure what for) when Sylvia began to softly snore. She hadn't been kidding about being tired.

So, in his brown pajamas, Sipowicz lumbered out into the living room, and fought the gnawing in his gut, that urge for a drink that didn't come as often as it once had but still did inevitably follow any emotionally wrenching episode. He crouched before the blue-green glow of his fish tank, and stared for a long time at his tropicals, lost in their gliding motion, their flashing in and around the coral, their almost neon colors—silver, yellow, purple, gold with paint slashes of white, rust-spotted brown—their dorsals flapping, ugly little faces on wedge-like waving forms, getting out of each other's way in their endless journey from one end of the aquarium to the other.

Were their travels any more or less pointless than his own?

Feeling sorry for himself, longing for a drink, he trudged over to the couch, flopped there like a fish out of water and stared at the ceiling, which wore the faint green shimmer of his burbling tank. Eventually he fell asleep.

Not deeply asleep, but deep enough that any preliminary noises in the outer hallway did not awaken him; it took the actual sound of wood splintering, dead bolt giving way, night latch popping free, to do that, as the front door of the Sipowicz apartment was opened by one good swift kick.

His eyes opened as suddenly as the door, the watery waves of fish-tank glow casting their eerie irradiation on the ceiling. He froze, knowing that his .38 in its holster was on his belt in the bedroom, knowing too that these intruders—their footsteps told him they numbered at least two—would not anticipate his presence on the couch.

In seconds that seemed eternal, he remained on his back, on the couch, waiting for them to move into view. He knew at once, without seeing them, that they were not thieves—thieves do not enter so dramatically, thieves do not enter so quickly. Their entrance was their signature: these were assassins.

Thank God for the fish tank, or the figure in the black turtleneck—round-faced, black-mustached, looking like Sipowicz's own stocky shadow—might have blended into the darkness, not fish-tank green, standing distinctly out, including his outstretched, black-gloved gun-in-hand. A nine millimeter.

Sipowicz grabbed the lamp from the endtable and hurled it at the moon-faced guy, a good hard pitch, and the sound of the lightbulb breaking was a brittle accompaniment to the bastard's yowl of surprise, which was echoed by Sylvia's own surprised scream, muffled behind the closed bedroom door.

"Stay put!" Sipowicz called to her. "Stay down!"

Noting another figure in black standing just inside, by the kicked-open door—skinny, hawk-faced—Sipowicz dove for the first guy, who had gone down on one knee from the blow of the tossed lamp; and the fat fucker was raising the nine millimeter to fire as Sipowicz landed on him, the gun going off just to Andy's side, thundercrack loud but not touching him, though an explosion of glass and a rushing of water told Sipowicz, without him seeing, that his precious fish tank had taken a slug.

Sipowicz was on top of the guy, and slammed a

fist into his fat face, and felt him go momentarily limp, allowing Andy to grab the nine millimeter from the would-be assassin's now flaccid grasp.

But shots were ringing out around him—the other man in black, the hawk-faced one, was punching holes in the plaster just above them.

And the bastard beneath him came suddenly alive, tossing Sipowicz off him, scrambling to his feet, as Andy went careening into the soggy rug where glass shards and wriggling fish made a uncomfortable landing pad. Somewhere along the way, Sipowicz lost the nine millimeter. His hand, empty of the gun, landed on a chunk of glass; the bullet that shattered the tank's glass had not put out the light within, and in a glow that was now yellowish not green, Sipowicz could see the perfect knife-like shard beneath his fingers.

And just above him was the second guy, the hawkish guy—only his eyes were small, snakelike—pointing an automatic down at him.

Sipowicz, gripping the glass shard, slashed with it, across the guy's arm, between the wrist of the hand that held the gun and his elbow. The shard cut Sipowicz's hand a little, as he gripped it; but mostly it ripped the fabric of the turtleneck and possibly fabric beneath and certainly skin, because a line of blood appeared as if Andy had drawn it and the guy yelped and lowered his arm, though not dropping the gun, and then the moon-faced guy was pulling his partner out of the apartment, their job left undone.

And they were gone.

Getting carefully to his feet, not wanting to step on any of his squirming pets, Sipowicz went to the light switch and threw it on, hollering, "It's okay, Sylvia! Come out!"

Briefly, he considered going after them; he glanced around, looking for the fumbled nine millimeter, didn't see it anywhere. And his .38 was still in the bedroom.

No, they were gone, Elvis had left the building, and Sipowicz's responsibility was here. With his family.

Sylvia appeared in the bedroom doorway in her nightgown, hand raised to quivering lips like the heroine of a gothic romance.

"Oh, Andy! What happened?"

"Those sons of bitches shot my fish tank."

"Your hand—should I call nine-one-one? The stationhouse . . . ?"

"That can wait," Sipowicz said, heading into the kitchen. "Draw some water in the tub."

Sylvia looked at him, incredulous. "You want me to draw a bath?"

"Yeah. Warm, not hot." He nodded toward his wriggling fish; their tails waved at the two humans. "We got lives to save."

And he went into the kitchen, wrapped his cut hand in a dish towel, and from the cupboard got a box of Ocean 50 sea mix.

TWO

Bobby Simone had hardly expected to return to the Sipowicz apartment so soon; nor did he expect, on his next visit to his partner's place, that he'd see a blue-and-white Crime Scene Unit station wagon parked out in front of Andy's building.

Simone had traded his earlier, casual attire for the sort of apparel he favored on the job—jacket and shirt and tie, in various shades of tan—because, though off duty, he was making this visit not just as a friend, but as a cop.

Coming in out of the surprisingly cool night (early morning, actually), the street slick and black from a brief rain and nearly deserted at two-fifteen, Simone met Greg Medavoy and Diane Russell on the stairs.

Simone was coming up, Medavoy and Russell coming down, and the three detectives froze in place and spoke for a while. Tall as he was, Simone was almost eye to eye with Medavoy, two steps up from him; Russell lay back, the awkwardness hanging in the air like humidity.

Simone acknowledged his former lover with a soft, "Diane."

And she said, with just a little edge, "Bobby."

Russell, undercover-casual in a burgundy polo, chinos, and hip-holstered .38, was poised two steps above Medavoy. Simone hadn't seen her lately. She looked good, if a little thin; she was the same lovely young woman he'd fallen for, with her perpetually tousled full head of brown curls, brown eyes that managed to be both direct and shy, and thin-lipped yet sensual mouth often caught in a near smile that seemed amused yet guarded.

Simone said to Medavoy, "I appreciate you callin' me at home, Greg."

Medavoy was forty-something, with reddish-blond hair, his regular features somewhat offset by startled-rabbit eyes. A good cop—and as conservative as his brown suit, white shirt, and striped tie—Medavoy's personal life was a disaster area, self-induced to some extent by hypochondria.

Like Russell, Medavoy—who for years had worked the Day Tour out of the 15th—had shifted over to Nightwatch because of a busted office romance. Unlike Russell, it had not been his idea.

Everyone in the squad knew that Lt. Fancy had wanted Medavoy separated from Donna Abandando. Medavoy had had a torrid, sometimes embarrassingly public affair with civilian employee Donna, the squad's receptionist. Donna's startling blond 'do was like something out of a 60s girl vocal group, but she was pretty and shapely and Simone always figured Greg was out of his league with her—though her rather garish taste in clothing was at least as questionable as her taste in men.

"N-no problem," Medavoy said. "I figured, hey, he's your p-partner, you'd wanna know if something bad went down."

"Nobody was hurt or anything," Simone said, "right?"

"Andy cut his hand on a piece of glass," Russell said. "Not serious."

Medavoy's grin was a nervous flinch in his face. "He used a fragment of his fish tank and slashed one of the intruders."

"There were two perps, right?"

"Right," Medavoy said.

"So how's Sylvia doing?"

"Better than Andy," Russell said wryly. She gestured with her head and the brown curls flounced. "Fancy's up there, trying to settle him down."

"Yeah," Medavoy said, "I thought I should call the Loo, when we caught this," then added, "as well as yourself."

"Loo can fill you in," Russell continued. "We got to get this building canvassed."

Simone nodded.

"We got four floors with three apartments per floor," Medavoy said, "and we got three floors done already, only nobody heard anything, is the story we're getting."

Russell's smirk was so cute it hurt. "Not even right across the hall from where Andy and Sylvia's door got kicked in."

"Wasn't it somebody in the building who called nine-one-one," Simone asked.

"Somebody with amnesia, apparently," Russell said, dryly.

Simone gave her a humorless smile, and a nod, and moved up the stairs past the two detectives as they moved down—and when he brushed by Russell, the familiar scent of her perfume, Bijan, and the slight contact of her shoulder brushing his arm was a moment as sweet to Simone as it was painful.

He showed his badge to the pair of uniforms at the doorway (the door itself was off its hinges and leaned up against the wall in the hall), then moved inside the apartment, where Lt. Fancy was trying to calm Andy down.

Simone hung back in the entry way, by the little hall in the kitchenette, just staying out of the way. Fancy had noticed him come in but Andy, whose back was to his partner, didn't.

"This ain't a freakin' crime scene, Loo," Andy was saying. "It's my apartment."

It was cool in the apartment, the air conditioner not having been turned down from earlier despite the coolness of the evening, but Andy was sweating like he was in a steam room.

Andy tossed his head toward the two-man investigation in progress and said, "If I wanted the Merry Maids in to clean up the place, I'da called 'em myself."

Two male detectives—their blue jumpsuits with CRIME SCENE UNIT stenciled boldly on the back—were at work in the disheveled little living room, one of them snapping photos, flash popping, another with his toolbox of equipment open beside him where he crouched near the floor by the skeletal framework of the fish tank, which still held a few jagged glass stragglers. A throw rug and some bare wood floor around the shattered fish tank were a mess, a mine-field of glass shards, thick with gunky residue from the chemically treated water.

"It's a crime scene, Andy," Lt. Fancy said quietly.

Arthur Fancy was a quiet man by nature, but his physical presence was loud; tall, broad-shouldered, with classically carved African-American features. Fancy was, like Simone, technically off duty, but also had taken time to wear his standard work apparel: a conservative gray suit.

Even Andy was dressed for work: short-sleeve checked shirt with a striped tie that in no way matched.

"Listen, Loo," Andy said, "can't you round these guys up and get 'em outta here? They're upsetting Sylvia. I won't have 'em getting her upset."

Sylvia, however, was standing calmly in the door-way of the bedroom, arms folded, leaning against the jamb, wearing a placid if faintly shell-shocked expression and a rust-colored robe with white lapels and a white cinched belt.

It was clearly Andy who was the agitated one.

"You call in CSU for homicides," Andy said. "No-body got killed here, except a spotted trunkfish and a scrawled cowfish."

Fancy did something he rarely did: blink. "What?"

Andy shrugged. "Couple fish I fell on. The spotted trunkfish, that won't be easy to replace. Not that you can replace any fish. I mean, these are specific fish."

"I'm sorry for your loss," Fancy said, and Simone, finally stepping into the room, was damned if he could read any sarcasm in it. "Calling in CSU was my idea, Andy. I got two men with guns breaking into the apartment of a police detective and an assistant D.A., what does that sound like?"

"Attempted homicide, to me," Simone said, popping a stick of gum in his mouth.

"Hey, Bobby," Andy said, looking dismayed except for eyes that were pleased, "you shouldn'ta got outta bed for this. Nobody got hurt."

Simone nodded toward Andy's right hand, which had a bloody handkerchief tied around it. "Looks like somebody did."

"You should see the other guy," Andy smirked.

Fancy said, "Andy managed to slash the right inner forearm of one of the assailants."

The CSU guy over by the fish tank said, "And we got fabric and blood samples."

"Nice," Fancy said.

"Somebody wants to do something constructive," Andy said, "they can make sure the ERs in town know about the new tattoo I carved that asshole."

"That's taken care of," Fancy said.

"Great, swell, peachy," Andy said. "Now why don't we clear everybody outta here. We can talk tomorrow, at the stationhouse. Right now I got things to do."

Simone said, "What kind of things, Andy?"

Fancy said, "He's going over to St. Luke's and get that hand checked."

"Are you kiddin', Loo?" Andy said, suddenly

falsely jovial. "I cut myself shavin' worse than this. Look, I got a mess to clean up, here, a floor to mop, a door to duct-tape shut, and fish to tend to—"

"Bobby," Fancy said, "you want to run him over there?"

"Glad to, Loo."

"I ain't leavin' Sylvia," Andy said.

"I'm glad to hear you mention her," Fancy said.

Andy's head jerked back. "What do you mean by that?"

Fancy's face was as expressionless as a manhole cover. "Well, all I been hearing about is fish."

Andy puffed up his chest. "That was uncalled for."

Simone said to his boss, "Has anybody taken a formal statement from Andy?"

"No," Fancy said.

"That can wait till tomorrow," Andy said.

"Why don't we gather Sylvia up," Simone suggested, "and go over and sit at the kitchen table, and just talk for a few minutes. I'll run a tape, and we got the household statement we need."

Fancy nodded. "Then you take Detective Sipowicz over to the ER and have that gash looked at."

"Does Detective Sipowicz get to have an opinion in this?" Andy wanted to know. "I had my house invaded here, gentlemen. First by those assholes, now by my fellow public servants. What's it gonna take to get some privacy back?"

Fancy gestured toward the kitchenette. "This."

Andy sighed his admission of defeat, shook his head in assent, and went over and collected Sylvia, taking her by the arm and walking her gingerly around the broken lamp, which one of the CSU investigators was dusting for prints.

"I told them rocket scientists the guy was wearin' gloves," Andy said disgustedly, as he guided his wife to a chair at the kitchen table. "Both of 'em was."

Bobby sat across from Sylvia; Fancy, appropriately enough, sat at the head of the table.

Sylvia said, "I can warm up some coffee."

"No," Fancy said, with a gentle smile. "That won't be necessary."

"Anybody got a great objection to me takin' a leak?" Andy asked. "Or would I be risking contaminatin' some key piece of evidence that Inspector Clouseau and Kato, over there, might run across?"

"Go ahead, Andy," Fancy said.

Andy trudged off to the john, and Simone asked, "How are you doing, Sylvia? You holding up? This kind of thing can be traumatic."

"I'm doing fine," Sylvia said, smiling warmly at him. "Bobby, you're not working tonight. You just came to show us support, didn't you?"

Simone smiled a little, nodded. "You guys'd be there for me."

"We're okay. Really." She looked sympathetically toward where her husband had exited. "He's just worried about his babies."

"His fish," Fancy said, faintly amused.

"That's what he's going in there for, right now," she said. "Checking on them."

"They're in the bathroom?" Simone asked.

She nodded. "Swimming around in the tub. Care-free. We should all be so lucky."

From the kitchen, the front door—or anyway, where the front door had been—was visible; and right now, Medavoy was making his way in, with Russell following.

"Loo," Medavoy said, "excuse me, but we got somethin' outta the canvass, finally."

"Good," Fancy said.

Russell edged beside Medavoy as the two stood at the kitchen table like delivery men who had interrupted a meal.

"Young couple on the first floor ordered a pizza," Russell said. "It was delivered within five minutes of the break-in, here."

Simone said, "You figure our two uninvited guests followed a delivery boy in?"

"Yeah, b-b-bluffed their way in or something," Medavoy said.

"Reach out for that delivery boy," Fancy said. "Maybe he can help us make an I.D."

Medavoy said, "The pizza place is closed, at this hour. We can check it out tomorrow, if you like, or if you rather turn it over to Day Tour—"

"I got a feeling we could use both of you back on days," Fancy said, "if you want to make the change."

Russell and Medavoy exchanged glances.

"I-I-I wouldn't mind," Medavoy said.

"You want me, you got me, boss," Russell said.

"I got a feeling," Fancy said, "that whatever this is, it comes out of the past. Our past. I think having people familiar with Andy, and his caseload, could be helpful."

Medavoy shrugged, grinned his nervous grin. "I'm up for it."

Russell nodded.

"I'll take care of it," Fancy said. "If you don't hear different, report at eight on Tuesday."

"We still got an apartment to check," Russell said. "Finish up."

Both Medavoy and Russell seemed pleased, and Russell and Simone found themselves caught in a quick but meaningful glance before the two detectives went back to canvassing the building.

Soon, Andy was back (Simone noted that there had been no sound of a flush), and sat opposite the lieutenant. The four of them might have been preparing to play a game of cards.

"Tell me exactly what went down, Andy," Simone said, placing his small cassette recorder on the table, pressing Record, and taking a few notes for his own benefit.

Andy told his story and Sylvia covered her mouth when Andy described looking up at the man pointing the gun at him. Though it was Andy's way to downplay, the bare bones of what had happened to him were nonetheless chilling to hear.

Andy's lip was lifted in a small sneer, but it contained a world of wrath. "I got a pretty good look at the sons of bitches. Couldn't make either of 'em, goddamnit. If they're local, I never run across 'em before. But we'll be old friends next time I see 'em."

"You could sit down with a sketch artist," Fancy said, "and come up with something solid?"

"Absolutely."

"Both perps?"

"Abso-freakin'-lutely."

Fancy said what Simone was thinking: "It's very obvious this is not a simple home invasion, gone awry."

Andy said nothing; his mouth twitched on the left side of his face.

Simone clicked off the tape recorder and said, "This was a hit, Andy."

Andy's eyes were hollow; his face was blank. "I know." Then he leaned over and touched his wife's hands—they were folded before her on the table—and said to her, "I'm sorry."

She seemed almost startled by that. "Sorry?"

"My line of work, you piss people off at you. Spills over into your private life, in nasty ways, sometimes. Maybe I, we, shoulda considered that, before we took this step—"

"Step? Getting married, you mean?" Her smile was mostly amused, but maybe just a touch irritated. "What about my line of work, Andy? You arrest criminals, but I prosecute them."

"We need to look at *both* your past cases," Fancy said.

"These guys were pros," Simone said.

"You think this is an O.C. hit?" Fancy asked Andy.

That was department shorthand for organized crime.

Andy's shrug was elaborate. "They was sure the

type. Nine millimeter automatics. Come in like fuckin' ninjas, all in black, ready to rock and roll. Military precision. If I hadn't been on the couch, they mighta done their thing and been in and out in a matter of seconds."

Sylvia was trembling.

Andy's eyes flashed with rage, and frustration. "But who the hell'd sic button guys on *me*? When's the last time I worked a major mob case, anyway?"

"Giardella," Sylvia said. Her face was very pale.

"Alfonse Giardella is dead," Simone said, speaking the obvious for everyone there, but needing to get the name out on the table. Simone knew little about the mutual vendetta the mob pornography king and Detective Andy Sipowicz had carried out a few short years ago; it predated his coming to the 15th squad.

He did know, from his time working in the police commissioner's office, when the case was of citywide concern, that Andy's partner John Kelly had been shot, seriously wounded, by a Giardella button man while he and Andy were guarding a key grand jury witness.

"Alfonse, may the wig-wearing scumbag hump rest in peace, is as dead as last week's veal," Andy said. "His fellow goombahs whacked him out, for rollin' over on 'em."

Fancy was nodding. "And they have a new element in there now, a younger regime, who were glad to see him go. If anything, the new group's probably grateful to Andy for helping get rid of somebody they saw as old guard."

Simone was tapping his pencil against his notebook. "Who else might have the hots for you, Andy?"

Andy threw a hand in the air. "Jeez, Bobby, you know the kinda cases we been catchin' lately. Routine shit. Lowlife pimps, drug dealin' skels, run-of-the-mill scumbag pus-pimples, your occasional domestic abuse situation that O. J.'s on ya . . ."

"Wait," Fancy said, raising a hand like a crossing guard. "Maybe we're overlooking the obvious."

Andy frowned. "Which would be what?"

Fancy spoke slowly, enunciating each word for its full effect: "J. Michael Wynn."

The name was a bomb Fancy had dropped, but that bomb lay between them unexploded, ticking ominously.

Fifty-five years old, movie-star handsome, heir to the Wynn insurance fortune, J. Michael Wynn had for years been the most popular rich guy in town, a society page regular, sort of like Donald Trump only not despised.

Wynn—who had never really worked a day in his life—contributed to charity, was a key contributor to the Democratic Party on local, state, and national levels, served on the boards of hospitals, universities, museums, and several of his family's companies. As a younger man, out of college, he was considered quite a playboy and got a lot of media, particularly when he dated movie stars like Angie Dickinson and Jill St. John.

In the late 1960s, he had married starlet Vicki Landon (who switched to "Victoria" immediately thereafter), and their storybook "Lifestyles of the Rich and

Famous" marriage had a surprise unhappy ending, last year, when Mrs. Wynn was found slashed to death in her kitchen at home.

This had ended Wynn's decades-long honeymoon with the public, who—along with the police—almost immediately branded him the murderer. Which seemed to Simone, and everyone else at the table, a very good call. After all, Wynn had a clearly trumped-up alibi, mysterious cuts on his hands, and blood thought to be the murderer's found at the scene was a DNA match-up with Wynn's own.

However, just under three weeks ago, J. Michael Wynn had been found innocent of murdering his wife, Victoria.

And Sylvia Costas Sipowicz had been the prosecutor.

"But Wynn's 'dream team' got him off," Andy said, wincing skeptically. "The rich psycho fucker walked!"

"I *lost* the case, remember," Sylvia said softly. "Why would someone like Wynn, who has everything, go after somebody he already defeated?"

"Maybe because he does have everything," Simone said. "If he's the kind of guy who can butcher his own wife—and get away with it, *and* live with it—maybe he does things just because he can."

"Sylvia," Fancy said, "you ran a very vigorous prosecution. And a fairly public one."

"I know I was criticized by some," Sylvia said, slightly defensive, "for trying the case in the media. But Wynn had all the funds in the world; we didn't."

"He got off!" Andy insisted. "He's 'not guilty,'

now and forever, and he's passed through the court system like a Taco Bell enchilada."

Andy was right: the late Victoria Wynn's parents were deceased and she'd had only one sibling, her sister, Constance, who was firmly in Wynn's camp. Wynn would not face the sort of civil trial that O.J. Simpson had.

Still, Simone was starting to think the lieutenant had something.

"Andy," Simone said, forcefully but not confrontationally, "Wynn got off, yes, and he was found not guilty by that jury—but not by the public and the media. To them, he's *guilty*, now and forever."

Andy made a face. "And he's gonna rehabilitate himself with the public by killing the prosecutor who tried his ass? I don't buy it."

"Listen to yourself," Simone said. "Andy, Wynn could have done this thing, and then pleaded his case in public just the way you are. His PR blitz would paint you as the target, drag out the old Giardella mob vendetta, make you out as some Dirty Harry who finally got his."

Sylvia was considering it. "Wynn did give some pretty bitter interviews, after the verdict, about my conduct on the case."

"He certainly can afford to buy his revenge," Fancy said. "As easy as picking up another Picasso or Porsche."

"Naw," Andy said, shaking his head. "No way."

But Andy Sipowicz was thinking. Simone could see it in the rapidly moving eyes in that putty mask. Andy said very little after that, and as Simone drove him over to the St. Luke's Roosevelt Hospital ER, the eyes kept moving and the putty mask hardened into stone.

The two men went alone. Sylvia had wanted to accompany her husband to the hospital, but he insisted she stay and keep an eye on his fish. And Sipowicz asked Fancy to stay and keep an eye on his bride, till he got back. The lieutenant obliged.

Andy got two stitches in his palm.

"Good thing I'm married and don't need this right now," he said, making a jack-off gesture, as he and Simone walked back out into the St. Luke's Roosevelt parking lot.

Simone stopped his partner with a gentle hand on the arm. Almost delicately, he said, "Andy, you gotta ask yourself this—if the mob didn't send those two, who else could access, who else could *afford*, that kind of talent?"

Andy raised his eyebrows in a facial shrug, and smiled like a mustached cherub.

"Well if it's who you guys think it is," he said, "all the gold in Fort Knox ain't gonna save J. Michael Wynn when I rip the heart out of his chest and feed it to him. . . . Listen, you think the Loo would mind if I come in a little late, t'morrow? I gotta get to Tony's Tropicals and pick up a new tank."

"I'm sure he'll understand," Simone said, and drove his partner home.

THREE

At 321 Fifth Street between Second and Third Avenue, a weatherbeaten six-story graystone squeezed between two even more nondescript buildings housed the 15th Precinct, which served and protected portions of the East Village, Little Italy, and Chinatown. Just across the narrow street past a row of slant-parked squad cars, the kids of I.S. 27 were enjoying mid-morning recess in the shade of trees not yet browned by fall, on a schoolyard where not long ago an eleven-year-old had been shot for standing on the wrong segment of cement.

No one was safe in this city, not even kids across the street from the police station. Not even cops sleeping at home on their sofa after a little spat with the wife.

Andy Sipowicz, anger burning in him like an ulcer, fended off with a wave and a word or two ("Sylvia's fine—thanks") the concerned inquiries of the several uniforms milling outside before he pushed open the double wooden doors into the stationhouse. Inside, as he moved through the bustle of the high-ceilinged reception area and past the Sarge behind his tall desk

("Hell of a thing, Andy,"), Sipowicz nodded and smiled tightly and kept his head down, pretending not to hear the more detailed queries and heading up the chain-linked stairwell.

Room 202, at the top of the stairs, was home to the 15th Detective Squad, a shabby world of water-spotted ceilings, shorting-in-and-out fluorescent lighting, and ancient cracked linoleum tile, where typewriters out-numbered computers, Rolodexes were a detective's weapon of choice, and institutional green walls were one big bulletin board of dog-eared mug shots, ragged crime-prevention posters, frayed street maps, and crookedly hanging framed photos of the NYPD chain of command.

To the right, against the smudged windows, was the church pew–like catching bench, free at the moment of distressed citizens; to the left, behind the rail, was receptionist Donna Abandando at her desk, with its quaint clutter (troll doll, miniature Stanley Cup and framed family photo—of her dogs).

"Good morning, Detective," Donna said, her voice as sweet as her smile, her blue eyes soft with sympathy.

Sipowicz smiled back at her, a little, appreciating her tact, not bothering him with questions and "support." Donna was one savvy cookie, even if she did dress like a sofa in a San Francisco whore house (this clothing critique was coming from a detective resplendent in brown jacket with blue and red tie and yellow-and-black checked shirt).

He lumbered through the gate in the railing to his desk, behind which loomed the green chalkboard duty roster. His desk, butted up against Simone's (empty at the moment), reflected his seniority on the squad: his was the closest to the door of the unisex bathroom/locker room. Slinging his jacket over the back of his chair, he settled in at the desk, covered his face with a hand, and considered calling his AA sponsor.

Adrianne Lesniak was at what had been Medavoy's desk, over by a wall of the glass-and-wood office where, through the open blinds, Lt. Fancy could be seen, on the phone, at his desk. Lesniak, a fairly recent addition to the squad, a pleasant-looking brunette in her late twenties with a nice build on her, looked up and smiled.

"Tired of well-meaning questions?" she asked.

"Does the Pope shit in the woods?" Sipowicz asked.

"Is a bear Catholic?" she responded, and returned to her paperwork.

Bobby Simone, buttoning a cuff of his tan shirt, his tan knit tie swinging, came out of the locker room and almost smiled, almost frowned. "Andy. How's the fish?"

Sipowicz knew Bobby's interest in his pets was not feigned, not mere politeness. Bobby bred pigeons, racing and homing; Sipowicz could appreciate a guy who liked animals, even though he himself would never have anything to do with such filthy creatures as pigeons.

"Happy as clams," Sipowicz said. "All I needed was a new tank. Filter, pump, heater, not a scratch."

Bobby ambled to his desk, but didn't sit. "That's good. How about your place?"

"Super was putting a new door on when I left. This time with a dead bolt that don't date to the Harding administration. Says he'll plaster up the bullet holes tomorrow."

"That's service."

"One of the few perks for bein' on the job: a cop in a building gets took care of . . . even if the neighbors did pull a Kitty Genovese on me."

Sipowicz was referring to a fabled case in the city, where the cries for help from a woman being murdered went unanswered, a New York City benchmark in citizens not getting involved.

"Gunshots don't always bring out the best in people," Bobby said. "Uh, the Loo wanted to talk to us, together, when you got here."

"Well, this is as 'here' as I get," Sipowicz said, getting up.

They moved toward the Lieutenant's office. Fancy was still on the phone, so they lingered just outside.

"You're starting that security thing tonight?" Sipowicz asked his partner.

"Yeah. Harry sends his regards, by the way."

The private investigative firm Bobby was working for was run by an ex-cop, Harry Timmons. Timmons was big on giving cops security gigs as night work.

Sipowicz, hands in pants pockets, rocked on his feet. "Harry still holds a good opinion of me, you think?"

"Sure, Andy. Why?"

"Nothin'. Loo's off the phone."

Fancy was waving them in.

Bobby went in first and Sipowicz shut the door behind them. Fancy's small office was the tidiest area in the cluttered squadroom, which wasn't saying much. The lieutenant was out from behind his desk, closing the blinds—something he rarely did. Sipowicz and Simone glanced at each other, wondering why the Loo felt he needed the extra privacy.

With a friendly smile that wasn't all that frequent a visitor to the lieutenant's face, Arthur Fancy said, "Sit down, Andy. Bobby."

They did.

Fancy got back behind his desk. He had his jacket off, was in shirt-sleeves and a striped tie in various shades of blue, which was about as casual as the Loo got.

Sipowicz shifted in the hard chair. "Hey, uh, thanks for the personal time this morning, Lieutenant."

"No problem. Sylvia?"

"She says she's fine." Sipowicz shrugged with his eyebrows. "She went in to the office today. I asked her not to, but there was no talkin' to her."

For some reason, that seemed to amuse Bobby a little.

Fancy was nodding. "Probably the best thing. Keep her mind off it. Got your fish squared around?"

"They're out of the tub and back in their own better world."

"Good."

Fancy's smile disappeared, signaling small talk was over.

"We've got the pizza delivery kid in the house," Fancy said.

"When can we talk to him?" Sipowicz asked.

"James took his statement."

James was James Martinez, youngest officer in the squad, who transferred from Anti-Crime two years or so ago. Good, smart, eager young cop.

Sipowicz asked, "Anything?"

Fancy leaned back in his chair, made a tent of his fingers. "Panned out just like we thought. Andy, an individual matching the description of the man you scuffled with—the stocky one with the mustache— followed the delivery kid into the vestibule, and was fumbling for his keys when the kid got buzzed through."

"And the kid wasn't suspicious?"

Fancy shook his head, no. "The guy made conversation with the kid, who said the guy seemed pleasant enough. White, middle-aged. Well-spoken. Clothing indicated he was fairly upscale. Held the door open for the kid."

Bobby asked, "You need somebody to run this kid down to the Big Building, to put him with a sketch artist?"

The Big Building was One Police Plaza.

"I made that call first thing," Fancy said, "and they sent their best man to us."

"Willets?" Bobby asked.

Fancy nodded. "He's sitting with the kid, now, in Interview One."

"I wanna see that masterpiece when they're done,"

Sipowicz said, pleased that the brass downtown were
taking the matter seriously.

Fancy shook his head, no. "Not till after you and
Willets have collaborated on your own artwork."

"I'm up for that," Sipowicz said. He allowed a
nasty little smile to form and gave both Bobby and
the Loo a knowing look. "Then I think we should
make a little high society–type call on J. Michael
Wynn."

Fancy frowned. "Who should?"

"Bobby and me." Sipowicz sat forward, locked his
hands. "I don't mind admitting I was full of shit last
night. Maybe I didn't like having the shoe on the
other foot."

"Who would?" Fancy said.

"Normally, I go with my first instinct on things.
But I give it a lot of thought . . . didn't sleep much
last night, after the place finally cleared . . ."

"That's only natural," Fancy said.

". . . and anyway, I thought about it and I come
around to your way of thinking, Loo. What you said
about Wynn makes a lot of sense. I guess it's that
macho thing, you know, made me think *I* had to be
the target of all that attention. But I see now it's
more likely Sylvia they was after. And I like Wynn
for why."

"I agree that Wynn's a suspect," Fancy said.

Sipowicz exchanged a confused glance with Bobby.
"What do you mean, you agree? You're the one came
up with it."

Fancy sighed. He rocked in his swivel chair, gently.

Calmly, slowly, softly, he said, "You and Bobby can't work this case, Andy."

Sipowicz flew to his feet. "You can't be serious—you can't expect me to sit by, not doin' dick, when some rich bastard sends out Lee Harvey Oswald and James Earl Ray to whack my wife—"

Bobby's hand was on Sipowicz's arm. Gently.

"Loo," Bobby said, reasonably, with that disarming little-boy smile in the midst of that Latin Lover mug of his, "I know it's not department policy to work a case you're personally involved in, but I promise you, I'll be there every step of the way with Andy. I won't let this go over the line—"

Offended, Sipowicz pulled his arm away from his partner's grasp. "You mean, you won't let *me* step over the line—"

"Sit down, Andy," Fancy said.

"Maybe I think better on my feet."

"Sit down, Andy," Bobby said.

"I can talk for myself," Sipowicz said, but sat.

"Bobby," Fancy said, "you can't work this case, either. You're too close to it to be objective."

"Loo," Bobby said, "I think I deserve a little more credit, little more respect, than—"

"It's not my call," Fancy said. "If I let you two work the case, I'd be as far out of policy as you are. We'd all wind up suspended."

"That's bullshit," Sipowicz said.

"I spent most of this morning on the phone," Fancy said dryly, "talking to people who are more important than we are."

Sipowicz snorted. "I'm surprised at you, Lieutenant. Don't you know everybody's created equal in this country?"

Fancy raised both palms; it was a calming gesture, but there was firmness to it—like a traffic cop.

"I got very little straddle to offer you on this, Andy," Fancy said. "You got to stay on the fringes of this thing. You're a witness, you're an information source . . . and I want you to maintain constant rhythm with the case detectives, but . . . you're *not* working the case."

Sipowicz twitched a sneer. "And who *are* the case detectives?"

"What I put in motion, last night," Fancy said casually. "Medavoy and Russell, back on days."

"Makes sense," Bobby said quietly. "They're the ones caught the case, after all."

Sipowicz glared at his partner. "What, now you're on his side?"

Fancy said, "We're all on the same side, Andy. You think J. Michael Wynn is some street skel you can slap around? Can you imagine how jammed up you could get yourself?"

Sipowicz waved that off. "This ain't my first time at the rodeo."

The lieutenant's eyes tightened. "You approach a man like Wynn with that distinctive style of yours, and you'll have one of the richest men in the city bringing police harassment charges that will embarrass the department and could cost you your career."

Sipowicz flew to his feet again, leaned across the desk and got right in Fancy's face. "There were guys with guns in my apartment last night, Lieutenant! If it was you and Lillian and your girls, and they come after you, come in your house like that, what the hell would you do?"

Unruffled, Fancy looked Sipowicz in the eyes and said, "Kill them with my bare hands, if I was able to . . . when they were in my house. The next day, I would turn it over to more objective hands."

Sipowicz was about to say, "Bullshit" again, but looking at the hard carved mask of Fancy's, he knew the lieutenant was telling the truth. He got out of Fancy's face and stood and stared at the window that would have looked out on the bullpen had the blinds not been drawn.

Fancy's voice was as calm as his words weren't. "Do you want yourself, and Sylvia, in the middle of a media storm? That's what will happen, if you go around rattling Wynn's cage. Right now, what happened last night is on the record as an attempted armed robbery."

Sipowicz blinked, turned away from the blinds and faced his boss. "That's how the sixty-one reads?"

A 61 was a complaint report.

"Yeah," Fancy said, "and Medavoy and Russell's DD-5 reads the same. So far, nobody from the media's got wind of it. Imagine what your life would be like, and how it would impact this investigation, if the *News*, the *Post*, the TV stations, knew there'd been an attempted hit on you and Sylvia: 'the cop the mob tried to kill' . . . 'the assistant D.A. who prosecuted the Wynn case'. . . ."

Sipowicz threw a hand in the air. "But, damnit, I can't just sit—"

Fancy leaned back and folded his arms and his eyes drew an unblinking bead on Sipowicz. "That's exactly what you're going to do, Andy. I want you to go back over every case you've worked since you—"

"Aw, shit, Loo!" Sipowicz slapped the air. "You got any idea how many scumbags I've sent to Riker's in my time?"

"My point exactly. We don't know for sure Wynn is behind this." Fancy shifted his gaze to Simone. "Bobby, I want you to reach out to the D.A.'s office and look at every criminal case Sylvia has prosecuted."

"I can do that," Bobby said.

"Andy, check with B.C.I. on every possibility you come up with, find out who's still inside that you— or Sylvia—sent there, and who's back on the street with a possible grudge."

Sipowicz grunted. "Ass duty."

The lieutenant's shrug was barely perceptible. "Only as relates to this case. You and Bobby will be catching other cases as they arise . . . to help Medavoy and Russell stay clear to concentrate on this."

Sipowicz's smile was tight across his teeth. "So while some filthy rich wife-murdering psychopath is fitting me and mine for the boneyard . . ."

Bobby slumped in his chair, covering his eyes.

". . . my partner and me are handling community policing logs, filing stop-and-frisk reports, takin' calls from citizens who think the Martians installed a radio receiver in their skulls—"

That marked the end of Fancy's patience.

"This isn't up for discussion," he said coldly. "That's all."

Outside the lieutenant's office, Sipowicz said, "He's supposed to stand up for us."

Bobby said, "Come on, Andy. It's policy. He's giving us more straddle on this than he should. You think Greg and Diane are gonna freeze us outta this?"

"No," Sipowicz admitted.

"Okay, then. Let's get to work."

He smirked disgustedly. "You don't really think we're gonna find some big surprise going back through old cases?"

"No. But it's got to be done. We are workin' the case."

"Yeah—the 'fringes.' "

But before long, Sipowicz was in Interview One with the police sketch artist, Willets, and after about an hour and a half, portraits of both intruders were finished and ready for circulation within the department. Most important would be the CATCH Units, in Staten Island, Brooklyn, and Queens; these units (the acronym stood for Computer Assisted Terminal Criminal Hunt) had photograph files cross-referenced according to age, height, etc.

The portrait Willets had drawn to the pizza kid's specifications of the stocky mustached intruder (who resembled Andy a little, except more hair and closer-set, smaller eyes) was almost identical to the Sipowicz-directed sketch.

This was, at least, progress, and Sipowicz was feeling pretty good when Sylvia—who was in the building taking a statement from a suspect on a domestic violence case—dropped by the squadroom.

"Want to get some lunch?" she asked him, the railing between them. She wore a short-sleeved cream-colored suit with a brown silk blouse; nobody was better than Sylvia at looking feminine and business-like at the same time.

"Sure," Sipowicz said. "Chinese?"

"Fine."

Soon they were in a rear booth at the Golden Dragon sharing appetizers and an order of Princess Shrimp. He filled her in on the events of the day— replacing the fish tank, the new apartment door, the frustrating meeting with Fancy, the satisfying police-artist sketches—and finally broached a subject that he knew would be hotter than the Szechuan-style shrimp.

"How's the hand?" she asked.

"Aw, it's fine. Hardly notice it."

"Good."

"You remember Harry Timmons?"

She was nibbling a fried wonton. "Um, security guy? Former officer? Didn't John Kelly do some work for him?"

"Yeah, and that's who Bobby's doing his night work for."

"Ah." She sipped her tea.

"I used to be pretty tight with Timmons." He bit the end off an egg roll. "Owes me favors."

She had that twinkle in her eye that she got when she knew he was leading up to something. "Thinking of collecting one?"

"Actually, yeah. I'm thinkin', maybe you should take some personal leave . . . for a week or two . . . till we know where we stand on this thing."

She frowned in confusion. "What do you mean?"

He took a healthy bite of the spicy shrimp, which cleared his sinuses. Eyes watering, he said, "It's just, I think stayin' home and lettin' me arrange for a, you know, some company for when I'm not there—"

Her expression froze. "A bodyguard."

"Yeah, you could call it that."

She put her chopsticks down. "Andy—home was where we almost got killed. Why would that be the safe place to go?"

He spoke through another bite of shrimp. "I don't think they'd try again at the apartment. I think with protection, that's the best place, most secure place to be."

She leaned back and folded her arms. "You mean, safer than at my office, or in the courthouse. Like, maybe I'll be standing in front of a jury and these hitmen will come crashing through the windows on ropes with Uzis?"

"This is serious, Sylvia."

Now she unfolded her arms and leaned forward; she spoke softly, not unkindly. "Andy—we don't know what that was about last night. We *think* we probably know . . . we think it's probably Wynn behind it . . . but it sounds to me like Lt. Fancy is going about handling the situation intelligently, and I'm not about to allow myself to behave like a helpless female, a frightened housewife . . ."

He was the one frowning, now. "Hey, I ain't askin'

ya to quit your job, give up your career, and play Betty Crocker! This ain't no half-assed feminist issue. It's a safety issue."

Her eyes narrowed and an edge came into her tone. "Are you staying home? Or are you going into work?"

"Of course I'm goin' to work—"

"Tell you what, Andy. I'll take personal leave, and you take personal leave. We'll stay home and protect each other, until this is resolved. We can even hire a bodyguard to protect us both, if you like."

"I'm not gonna do that—"

"Of course not. And I wouldn't ask you to."

He frowned. "So what was that, sarcasm?"

The patronizing smile she gave him was one of the few things he didn't like about her. "Yes. Don't you recognize it, coming from somebody's mouth other your own?"

And now she frowned, but it seemed more sad than angry.

"I treat you with respect, Andy. Treat me the same way. I'm late—have to get back."

And she got up and left him there with the bill.

FOUR

Bobby Simone had a ballet dancer's loose-limbed, fluid grace, and the self-possessed air of a Zen master. Tall and muscular as he was, he was nonetheless as well-coordinated as his dark green suit, light green shirt, and dark green patterned tie.

As a detective, he prided himself on his ability to deal with people from all walks of life. Though a wellspring of rage occasionally bubbled up, his easygoing self-confidence, tempered by shyness, even diffidence, almost never left him.

Almost.

Greeted by a gray-templed black butler in full livery at the door of a penthouse in one of the twin-towered apartment houses that gave Central Park West its distinctive skyline, Simone knew at once that he had entered a place where he did not belong, a world beyond his control, an environment outside his experience.

It was as if he had entered a mansion, not an apartment; or perhaps a museum, except that there was a studied sparseness to the displayed paintings and antiques, an effort to avoid clutter and achieve good taste.

"I'll announce you, sir," the butler said, in a cultured baritone.

"Yeah, thanks," Simone said.

A brass-and-wrought-iron–railed staircase curved to an open second floor underneath which a wide, square portal led to a formal living room, where the butler had disappeared. Simone waited in the foyer—the walls a cool, cream-colored marble block, the floor marble tile with a black diamond pattern—standing near a framed frieze of pudgy angels who floated above a low-slung gilt wood table bearing Chinese vases, Japanese boxes, and cut orchids. His only chaperon was a crystal chandelier that would have made a great earring for the Statue of Liberty.

There was a second reason, beyond all this intimidating opulence, for Simone's uncharacteristic unease.

This penthouse house apartment belonged to one J. Michael Wynn—the same J. Michael Wynn who, according to the consensus around the 15th Precinct, was almost certainly behind dispatching those hired killers into Andy and Sylvia's apartment.

The one and the same J. Michael Wynn who, according to Charles Grodin and Geraldo Rivera and the public at large, had slaughtered Mrs. J. Michael Wynn with a carving knife, leaving her to bleed to death on the kitchen floor of this very apartment.

And Simone was here to do a job for J. Michael Wynn.

Coincidences troubled Simone, but he was not about to look this particular gift horse in the mouth. Harry Timmons had asked Simone if he had any problem with working for Wynn, who after all was considered by every cop on the NYPD to be a textbook example of a rich scumbag who had bought himself a not guilty verdict.

"I know your partner's wife prosecuted him," said Timmons, the heavy-set, prosperous head of Gold Shield Investigative and Security Services. "And he said some pretty unflattering things about her, in the press, on the tube."

"*You* got a problem with me takin' the job, Harry? You think I won't be objective?"

"I don't care," Timmons had said. "He's a rat bastard wife killer, ain't he?"

And of course this conversation had occurred before the break-in at Andy's.

Initially, Simone figured he really would try to be objective and just do whatever job Wynn wanted done, unless it struck him as unsavory or something. And if Simone happened to stumble upon anything incriminating about Wynn, where the murder of Mrs. Wynn was concerned, well that would just be a bonus.

But now Simone viewed the Wynn job as an opportunity to do some no-holds-barred sub-rosa investigating on Andy's behalf. Of course he would have to keep this windfall from Andy, and from Fancy. If Andy knew his partner had access to Wynn, God only knew what excesses would transpire; and the Loo would consider Simone in violation of his order not to work the case.

So this had to be Simone's secret. The question

was, would Wynn recognize him as Andy Sipowicz's partner?

The butler returned, said, "Mr. Wynn will see you
in the study. . . . If you'll just follow me, sir," and led
Simone across a living room larger than 95 percent of
the apartments in Manhattan, past overstuffed sofas
and easy chairs of a creamy chenille arranged on a
vast oriental carpet, with footstools that wore tapes-
tries no shoe ought dare touch. The safari continued
past tall potted plants, with a modern metal sculp-
ture on a pedestal here, an antique English landscape
there, and, over the fireplace, a formal portrait in oils
of a very beautiful blonde woman in pearls and
peach gown—the late Victoria Wynn, who Simone
recognized from society page photos before her
death, and front-page photos after.

Still trailing the butler, Simone craned his neck to
take in the portrait of the dead woman (was it sick
to notice the lovely full bosom the painting showed
off, and to such a surprising degree?). When he again
faced forward, Simone felt almost as if he'd been
caught at something: the woman's husband, J. Michael Wynn, was suddenly headed toward him.

The butler fell back as Wynn, coming from the
study, met Simone not quite halfway, noticing the
detective taking in his surroundings.

"It's a bit of a hodge-podge, I admit," Wynn said.
"English, French, Italian, Oriental antiques mixed in
with a few modern things."

"A real United Nations," Simone said, with a little
smile, somehow relieved Wynn (apparently) didn't

realize Simone had been staring at his late wife's bosomy portrait.

Wynn offered his hand to Simone, with the unnecessary but gracious introduction, "I'm Michael Wynn."

Simone took Wynn's firm grasp. "Bobby Simone."

Though Simone made him at five-nine or ten, the slender Wynn seemed bigger; he had movie star–like presence, even if his matinee-idol face looked a little puffy. His medium-length, well-styled hair was a solid silver, his light blue eyes (under round-lensed designer wireframes) would have put Robert Redford to shame, his tan rivaled George Hamilton's, and his smile was as dazzling as Jack Nicholson's, only without the menace.

"Simone," Wynn said. "That's French?"

"Yes. My father was French, mother Portuguese."

"Speaking of United Nations," Wynn said cheerfully.

He wore a pale blue cashmere polo sweater with the sleeves pulled up, tan linen slacks, and suede oxfords. It was the sort of casual outfit that would have cost Simone a month's pay.

"Would you like something to drink?" Wynn asked. "Coffee? Iced tea, perhaps?"

"No, that's fine."

Wynn glanced toward the butler and said pleasantly, "Then, that'll be all for the moment, George."

Simone followed Wynn into the study, where the marble walls gave way to blond wood paneling and a parquet floor with a plush beige rug; vintage equestrian paintings in gilt frames hung here and there.

At right, next to a wall of windows whose white shutters were shut tight, was a blond modern desk as big as a small car, with blotter, phone, and appointment book, but nothing else. Nothing in the room—hell, in this entire apartment—looked as if anyone had ever used it.

Wynn headed toward a dark green velvet-cushioned sofa that sat against a wall that was a massive built-in floor-to-ceiling book case, containing as many art pieces as antique books.

"I like the Timmons agency," Wynn was saying, gesturing for Simone to take a needlepoint-tapestry armchair near the sofa, where he then sat himself. "All of his people are either ex-police officers or currently moonlighting ones. Which category do you fall into, Detective Simone?"

"The latter."

Wynn leaned back, crossed a leg over his knee, draped an arm along the upper sofa cushions. He seemed casual, at ease. Simone felt as stiff as the uncomfortable armchair he was sitting in.

"You might be surprised," Wynn said, "given my current . . . celebrity . . . that I would want to have an NYC cop working for me. Considering that most, if not all of them, think I got away with murder."

"I am a little surprised."

A half smile dug into Wynn's cheek; he had the kind of lines in his face that only underscored how handsome he was. "Well, any misgivings I might have about the likelihood of you or any officer having a bias toward me are outweighed by my need to have a truly qualified, professional individual working for me. With many security agencies, and private investigative firms, you have no idea what sort of man you're hiring."

"That's true."

In New York state, you only needed one private investigator's license to open up an office—and you could hire a hundred (or more) "investigators" and "private security officers" (no matter what their qualifications were or weren't) to work under that single license.

"I also think, Mr. Simone, that as you get to know me, you'll come to doubt that I killed Victoria."

Wynn might have been commenting on the weather.

Simone shifted in the uncomfortable chair. "The jury found you not guilty, Mr. Wynn. Who am I to second-guess them?"

"A seasoned professional." Wynn's smile was as disarming as it was white. *Caps?* Simone wondered.

"My understanding," Simone said, "was that this was a bodyguard job."

Wynn sat forward, put his hands on his knees; his expression was cool, except for an urgency in the spookily light blue eyes.

"If by that you mean," Wynn said, "what does my wife's murder have to do with what I'm hiring you for, you're correct. It is a bodyguard assignment, and it does have nothing to do with Victoria's death. But we needed to get that out of the way, didn't we?"

Simone shook his head, no. "Really wasn't necessary, Mr. Wynn."

Wynn's eyes tightened as he casually asked, "Do you know anything about my daughter? Laura?"

"Should I?"

"There have been articles about her. One in *People*, several locally. She's an actress."

Simone shrugged. "Maybe I did see something. Was she in a movie?"

Wynn seemed pleased by this near-recognition. "Supporting role in a Mel Gibson picture. She's done some television, too, things shot here in the city. Several small roles on soap operas. And she had quite a good part, last season, on 'Law and Order.' "

"Afraid I don't watch much television."

Wynn wore the glazed, slightly stupid smile that was a badge of parental pride. "Of course, her love is theater. She's very gifted. You would think being a child of wealthy, socially prominent parents would give her an advantage, but in some ways, I think it's been a roadblock." The smile was gone now; his forehead was tight with indignation. "She's run into prejudice. Resentment."

"That can happen."

Wynn rose, walked down to the place in the bookshelf, near his desk, where some framed family photos nestled between books and objets d'art. He plucked one framed picture from the grouping and came over and handed it to Simone.

"This is her."

It was a photo of Laura Wynn next to Mel Gibson taken on the street, on location, in the city somewhere; looked like SoHo, maybe. Gibson's smile was polite, but Laura's was radiant, the same dazzling smile her father could conjure up. She was a beauty—blonde, blue-eyed, like Michele Pfeiffer only not so skinny. She had inherited her mother's full bosom.

"Lovely young woman," Simone said, and handed the photo back to Wynn.

"She's the image of her mother," Wynn said, looking at the photo.

"I can see the resemblance," Simone said.

Wynn touched the rim of his wireframes. "Except, of course, Laura has my blue eyes. Victoria's were green."

"Well, she's very pretty."

Wynn returned the photo to its position on the shelf, returned to the sofa and sat, leaning back again.

And then he calmly came out with what at first seemed a non sequitur: "My wife was an alcoholic."

This Simone already knew. Stories had come out, in both the tabloid media and in court, about Victoria Wynn's drinking; in fact, witnesses had disclosed numerous examples of displays of Mrs. Wynn's vile, alcohol-fueled temper, which had been the only public chinks in the armor of their "perfect" marriage. She had been seen to strike her husband, on several occasions, and the prosecution's major murder theory was that Mrs. Wynn had finally struck Mr. Wynn once too often.

Though Wynn had been tried for first-degree murder, there were many who speculated that perhaps Victoria Wynn's killing had even been a bizarre sort of self-defense.

Rumors had flown about the prosecution floating a plea bargain on that basis, but Wynn had reportedly rejected it—a smart move, considering that he wound up winning all the marbles.

Wynn's voice was hushed; it was almost as if he were talking to himself, when he said, "Beauty was not the only thing my wife and daughter had in common, Detective Simone. Though Victoria and I weren't aware of it for some time, Laura began drinking in her early teens. I'm afraid in some respects, it's an old story, for people like us: Victoria and I alternately spoiled and neglected our daughter, our only child."

"You don't have to be well-off to do that."

Wynn smiled; there was irony in it. "Laura is a Yale grad—part of their repertory company, which is the best in the country—and she studied with the Circle Repertory Company's lab, too. . . . But her most recent accomplishment is to graduate, with honors, from the Betty Ford Clinic."

Simone leaned forward, resting an arm on his knee. "She's sober, now?"

"Yes." Wynn smiled again, no irony this time. "And her attitude is good." Now the smile faded. "But something's come up that's both a wonderful opportunity, for her, and, I fear, a potential pitfall."

"How's that?"

His mouth smiled while his forehead frowned. "She's landed a role in an off-Broadway play. It's a possibility she's being exploited, for her name, her fifteen-minutes-of-fame celebrity . . . but she is a very good actress, and this will be a chance for her to show what she can do, *if* the critics don't punish her for who her father is. . . . Are you familiar with the Marian Wald Theater?"

"Sure. On East Thirteenth."

A number of plays in recent years had graduated from the Marian Wald to Broadway. Most of the theaters in the Village, in fact most off-Broadway theaters period, did new plays, often by new, unknown playwrights; but the Marian Wald specialized in revivals, particularly obscure works by well-known playwrights.

"Laura has a leading role in the new production of a Maxwell Anderson play from the thirties," Wynn said. "It opens Friday—they're still in rehearsal. The play is scheduled for three weeks, but it could run longer. . . . Are you willing to take on the job?"

Simone frowned, puzzled. "What job?"

Wynn gestured toward Simone, with an open hand. "To be my daughter's bodyguard for the run of the play. Chauffeur her to the theater . . . accompany her to any after-show get-togethers with cast members she might want to go to . . . and then chauffeur her home."

"I don't much care for playing chauffeur, Mr. Wynn; I don't even own a car—"

"Rent one and add it to the bill."

Simone was shaking his head. "Excuse me, Mr. Wynn, but I must be missing something. Why would your daughter *need* a bodyguard?"

Wynn's chin was raised, his eyes hooded. "The ostensible reason is to protect Laura from *paparazzi* and other representatives of the tabloid media who might seek to exploit her and her mother's death."

"But that's just a pretext?"

Now Wynn's gaze was straightforward. "No, it's valid enough—but I am more concerned with you keeping an eye on her. Do I have to even mention, Detective Simone, that the world of theater is awash with substance abuse—and abusers—and not the ideal place for a recovering alcoholic?"

"You want to know if she's slipping off the wagon."

"Yes."

Simone was shaking his head, no. "I can't tell her not to drink, Mr. Wynn. Security work isn't babysitting."

"To some degree I would think it is, but no, you're not to play moral watchdog. But you are to report what you see, to me, and should she slip too badly off the wagon, obviously you would get her immediate medical attention. Think of yourself less as a babysitter and more as a safety net."

Simone considered that. "All right. I think I can do that for you."

Wynn beamed. "Excellent."

Simone held up a cautionary hand. "You understand I can only work evenings. If you want a 'chauffeur' for any matinees, you better check with Harry Timmons for a back-up."

"Understood."

"Where does your daughter live?"

Wynn gestured upward. "Here . . . but she's at a rehearsal, right now. Can you start tomorrow evening?"

"Yes."

"Wonderful." Wynn stood. "I'll see you out."

Wynn walked side by side with Simone through the vast expanse of living room, past the antiques of various countries, the modern art pieces, the portrait of the busty late Mrs. Wynn.

Placing a gentle hand on Simone's arm, Wynn said, as they walked, "As you can see, Detective Simone, any bias against me is irrelevant to this assignment. You don't have to believe in my innocence to protect my daughter."

Protect her from herself, he meant.

"You're right, Mr. Wynn."

They moved into the high-ceilinged foyer, where their footsteps—and voices—echoed off the marble.

Wynn escorted Simone to the door, saying, "And I want you to know that I do regret the things I said to the media about Sylvia Costas."

Simone froze. "What?"

Wynn's expression was almost contrite. "I just hope you'll understand how frustrated and bitter I was, in the aftermath of that ordeal. . . . Yes, I know that you're Detective Sipowicz's partner."

"And you still want me to work for you?"

And now Wynn's expression was blank—unreadable. "I requested you."

Simone felt like he'd been coldcocked. "Requested me?"

"Well—I requested a detective from the Fifteenth Precinct, since it covers the East Village. That's where my daughter's play is, after all. Mr. Timmons said the only man from the Fifteenth currently doing work for him was you—and he was straight with me about who you were."

Timmons hadn't been all that straight with Simone, however, had he?

Simone said, tightly, "And you told Timmons you wanted me, anyway."

Wynn shrugged. "After I did some checking up on you."

"Really?"

"I do my homework, Detective Simone. You have an exceptional record with the department. Several medals of valor. One of the youngest men in the history of the NYPD to earn a gold shield, and the police commissioner himself has commended your work. But more important . . . and this is delicate . . . I hope you'll take no offense . . . but I knew we had something in common, you and I."

"What's that?"

"Sorrow." Wynn opened the door.

Simone stepped out into the hall, not completely understanding.

Wynn gave the final explanation: "You lost your wife, too."

And closed the door.

FIVE

Andy Sipowicz spent Tuesday morning at his desk in Room 202 at the 15th Precinct, wading through stacks of manila folders containing 61s and DD-5s and other heirlooms of cases dating back to the early 80s, from file cabinets around the squadroom and dusty boxes from storage in the precinct-house basement. These were artifacts that never had, and probably never would, be transferred to computer disc or microfiche—too little money, too many crimes, for the modern world to ever catch up.

Across from Sipowicz, Bobby Simone was engaged in a similar exercise, with materials provided for him by the District Attorney's office. Sylvia's cases didn't date back as far as Andy's, and Bobby had a smaller number to dig through; but the files were thicker.

Detectives Diane Russell and Greg Medavoy were back on Day Tour, starting today, but they'd only been in, momentarily, at the top of the morning; their empty desks were a nagging reminder to Sipowicz that somebody other than he and Bobby were in charge of the case.

The other two Day Tour detectives, Martinez and

Lesniak, were out on an armed robbery call. The
morning was otherwise quiet, with no walk-ins to
speak of, and pretty Donna—nicely filling out a
green sweater with sparkly appliqués that would
have been perfect for a Christmas party (of course,
this was freakin' *September*)—took the occasional
phone call, never once finding anything worthy of
passing along to the two detectives in the house.

It was a little before eleven.

"How do you like workin' hemorrhoid patrol?"
Sipowicz asked his partner, flicking a hand at the
stacked files. "Nothin' but piles and piles . . ."

"Beats directing traffic—I guess. You find anything interesting?"

Sipowicz waved a memo-size piece of paper. "I
got a list of under-achievers for B.C.I. to check out,
but we're really whippin' the skippy on this one.
These nickel-dime street skels we put away, on a
daily basis, gang kids and boost artists and such, you
picture them hiring hit men?"

Bobby laughed mirthlessly. "No. This is a mobbed-
up hit if I ever saw one."

Sipowicz nodded, slapped a pile of files. "And the
only wiseguy I can think of, with a big enough beef
against me to work up a revenge jones, is that late
unlamented asshole, Alfonse Giardella."

Bobby's brow knit in thought. "You think he might
have friends or family who could have picked up
the torch?"

Sipowicz shook his head, no. "He didn't have any
kids—God in His infinite wisdom musta made that
prick sterile. His widow lives in Atlantic City in a

condo, well-fixed, stuffin' Alfonse's estate into slot machines a silver-dollar at a time, and playin' Keno."

"She was his secretary, wasn't she?"

"Yeah, he had another wife that died. No kids by that marriage, either. Some young cousin of his winded up takin' over the porn business."

Bobby nodded. "Angelo Giardella."

"Right. Word is the kid is steerin' clear of prostitution and underage talent. More your clean-cut pornographer type of guy."

"I heard the same thing," Bobby said. "NYU grad takin' over the family business."

Which just happened to be adult bookstores, peep shows, hardcore pornography, and strip clubs. But apparently without Alfonse Giardella's ties to drug trafficking and fencing operations.

"How about you?" Sipowicz nodded toward Bobby's stack of folders. "You come up with anything?"

Bobby shook his head, no. "Sylvia's mob-related cases were few and far between."

"She coulda told ya that."

"She did. I'm making a list for B.C.I. to check, myself, but it's pretty pointless. Nothing here that would spark that kind of retaliation."

Sipowicz pointed to Bobby's stack of files. "You didn't happen to run across a rich guy in there, who killed his wife with a carving knife and got away with it?"

Bobby smiled faintly. "I think maybe I did, now that you mention it."

Sipowicz smirked. "Russell and Medavoy are over

at Wynn's Central Park West address, talking to that fourteen-carat slimeball right now."

"I would expect."

"It ought to be us talkin' to him."

"I know."

Bobby was starting on another file.

"Speaking of the upper classes," Sipowicz said, "I forgot to ask you. How'd that bodyguard gig turn out? Wasn't that supposed to be for some rich asshole?"

Bobby didn't look up from the file. "Yeah . . . Interesting. Starts tonight."

"Thought you started last night."

"That was a preliminary meeting."

Sipowicz nodded. "Size you up kinda thing."

"Yeah."

"So what's the gig? Or am I pryin'?"

Bobby shrugged. "Rich guy's daughter needs a bodyguard."

"Little kid?"

"No. Like, twenty-five."

"Good-lookin' girl?"

"I haven't met her yet, but she photographs nice."

Sipowicz plucked the next file off his stack. "Sounds like a tough way to make an extra buck. Maybe I oughta give Timmons a call."

"You're already in a two-income family."

"Yeah. My wife and me both got jobs that make people want to murder you."

Bobby looked up with a concerned frown. "So how is Sylvia doing?"

"I wouldn't know. She ain't talkin' to me."

Shortly before noon, Russell and Medavoy came up the steps and into 202. Russell was in the lead; she wore dark sunglasses, a blue polo, and tan chinos and, but for the badge and gun on her hip, might have been a drug-dealing suspect. Medavoy, in his brown suit and yellow-and-red tie, was hauling in.

Sipowicz looked up sharply and said with his eyes, to Russell, *Anything?*

Russell opened the gate of the bullpen rail, saying to Medavoy, "Fill in the Loo, would you, Greg? I need to hit the head for a second."

"S-sure thing, Diane," Medavoy said, and headed for Fancy's office while Diane moved between Sipowicz's desk and the chalkboard duty roster. Sipowicz glanced up at her and, taking off the sunglasses, she gave him the slightest wag of her head, toward the locker room, where she went in.

"Gimme a second," Sipowicz said to Bobby, who had picked up on the signal.

"Sure," Bobby said. But he had that funny glazed-over look he got—half pissed, half lovesick—when Diane was around.

The locker room was a dingy yellowed-tile and green-plaster chamber of horrors that included toilets without lids, a low-slung cloudy mirror over a pair of sinks that dated to Mayor LaGuardia's term of office, a double tier of small rust-pitted dented lockers that weren't big enough for a junior high kid's school books, and a single shower stall with a cracked plastic curtain that made the Bates Motel shower seem inviting.

But it was also the squad's unisex john, meaning it had a lock that could provide privacy.

Sipowicz locked the door behind him and said to Russell, "So how was glamour boy?"

"J. Michael Wynn is one slick customer," Russell said. She was pacing. "You should see that place. Marble and antiques and money."

"He seemed surprised, when you told him about what happened to me and Sylvia?"

She stopped pacing, bit her bottom lip, raised an eyebrow. "Yeah. He seemed surprised. Even concerned."

Now Sipowicz was pacing. "That bastard."

"We showed him the suspect sketches, asked him if he'd ever seen these individuals . . . not the faintest indication in his eyes, his body language, demeanor, nothing to say he'd ever seen either of 'em before."

"He *hired* 'em!"

She raised a hand in a "stop" fashion. "Andy, it was a perfunctory interview. We didn't exactly expect him to crack."

"He did it."

"You're probably right."

Sipowicz glared at her. "Probably?"

She smiled, but there was nothing happy about it. "Andy, he's good. I interviewed a lot of bad guys, okay? I heard a lot of lies in my time, way more'n my share . . . and this guy is either one hell of an actor, or he really is innocent."

Sipowicz narrowed his eyes and pointed a finger at her. "Sociopaths ain't got a conscience, Diane.

They can look you in the freakin' eye and tell you up is down, black is white, dead is alive.''

She was pacing again; hanging her head. "I know. I know.''

Her eyes had dark circles, her attractive face seemed drawn, pasty white.

Sipowicz said, "You don't look so good.''

"I'm okay.''

"You hangin' in there?''

"Yeah. Yeah.''

She went over and leaned on the sink; looked at herself, then quickly looked away.

He stood beside her. "I know it's hard.''

"I been dry for six weeks, Andy.''

"That's good. That's real good.''

"But it hurts. I still want it.''

"I know.''

She looked around the grungy locker room. "This is where I used to come, Andy, to sneak sips.''

"One day at a time.''

She turned to him and her eyes were wet. "I . . . I want to see Bobby. I want to tell him what I've accomplished. I want him back in my life, Andy.''

"You think you're ready?''

". . . Yes.''

"You don't think you're ready.''

"I want him back in my life so bad, Andy.''

"When you get to where you want that more than a drink, we can consider this. You understand?''

She nodded. "Yes. . . . Let's go talk to the Loo. There's other news. Better news.''

"What?''

In the lieutenant's office, with Russell and Simone seated, Sipowicz and Medavoy standing behind them, Fancy—who remained seated at his desk throughout the meeting—held up a mug shot, side and front, of a round-faced mustached individual who looked just a little like Andy Sipowicz.

"*That's* the ugly son of a bitch," Sipowicz said. "That's the one I went tangle-ass with."

Simone asked, "One of the CATCH units come up with that?"

"Naw," Medavoy said, grinning, proud of himself, "it was Organized Crime Task Force. This wasn't computers—somebody actually recognized the guy."

"Lt. Waddell made him," Russell said. "Waddell picked him up here in ninety-one after Gotti's lieutenant was hit in that restaurant. Questioned and released."

"So this *is* a mob thing?" Simone asked. "It's not Wynn?"

"Could be mob," Fancy said, "could be Wynn. Could be something else."

Sipowicz twitched a sneer. "This shining example of mankind got a name?"

"Name's Leonard Parsons."

"Sure this is a mob hit," Sipowicz said, with withering contempt. "There's a real Eye-talian-American name for you—Leonard Parsons."

Fancy continued: "Chicago talent, but not aligned with any mob family there, or elsewhere, to anyone's knowledge."

"In fact," Russell said, "he's been a suspect in several non-mob hits disguised as home-invasions gone wrong."

"Two years ago, a murder in Chicago, candy manufacturing heiress who was killed," Medavoy said. "The husband made out like a bandit. The Chicago PD and the insurance investigators suspected murder-for-hire and liked Parsons for the hitter."

"No charges brought," Russell said.

"He's only done time once," Fancy said. "Joliet, for a straight home invasion. Eighty-four. Went away for thirteen months."

"Freelance talent," Sipowicz said.

Simone asked, "What about the other guy?"

"Waddell didn't make the second sketch," Russell said, "but that's no surprise."

Fancy lifted a file folder. "On every arrest in his package, Parsons was picked up alone . . . but Organized Crime doesn't believe he's a lone wolf. They're convinced he's working with a partner, a back-up, which is common among professional killers, particularly the freelance variety."

Simone asked, "Is anything known about the partner?"

Fancy lifted his eyebrows. "The police sketch off Andy's description is the first anybody's ever got on the partner. Till now, he's been a ghost."

"He's a ghost with a gash in his arm, now," Sipowicz said. "I hope it's infected."

"Maybe it is," Fancy said. "Nobody with a wound like that showed up at any ER in the city."

"Or in New Jersey, either," Russell added.

Simone picked the photo off Fancy's desk and had

a look. "What else do we know about Leonard Parsons?"

Fancy said, "Not much. The Chicago PD doesn't have a current address on him, but his package says he's got . . . refined tastes. He's into the finer things, gourmet dining included."

"Maybe his profession pays well," Sipowicz said. "Maybe he's got some well-to-do clients."

Fancy said, "Greg, Diane, I would suggest you canvass the tonier hotels and restaurants in Manhattan."

"That's a lot of ground to cover, Loo," Sipowicz said, eagerly, moving closer to Fancy's desk. "Maybe Bobby and me could help out—"

Russell said, "We've only scratched the surface where Wynn's concerned, Loo. We haven't talked to the sister-in-law yet, the one who alibied him. . . ."

"Lesniak and Martinez will help on the canvass," Fancy said, "as their caseload permits, and of course we'll send out circulars."

"What about us?" Sipowicz asked, glancing at Bobby.

"Back to the files," Fancy said.

Sipowicz said, "Hey, but we're almost done . . ."

Which was a lie.

Fancy's gaze moved from Sipowicz to Bobby and back again. "Then reach out to B.C.I. and get your lists of possible suspects run. You want to get back on the street, that's how."

"Thanks, Loo," Sipowicz said, the two words dripping more sarcasm than two words should be asked to convey.

"Don't mention it," Fancy said.

SIX

Simone, once again ushered in by the butler, stood in the marble foyer in the shadow of the magnificent chandelier, as if he were awaiting a debutante to come sweeping down the curving staircase in a ballgown. He might have been underdressed for such an occasion, in his dark blue suit with light blue shirt and blue-and-charcoal striped tie; but when his "date" did come down the stairs, former debutante that she was, she made him look positively formal.

In a black turtleneck and black jeans and clunky black boots, Laura Wynn—shapely, rather small—came clomping down the stairs with what seemed a defiant, deliberate lack of grace. She wasn't as lovely as in the photo of her with Mel Gibson—the honey blond hair was back in a ponytail, her pretty face bare of makeup save for smidges of mascara and lipstick—but she was still lovely enough. The light blue eyes were striking and a little scary.

"Well, at least you're not hard on the eyes," she said, looking him up and down, frankly. Her voice was a throaty purr but her tone was brittle. "I was expecting somebody older, fatter, and rougher around the edges."

"Hope you're not disappointed, Miss Wynn," Simone said, and extended his hand. "Bobby Simone."

Her handshake was firm, her flesh cool.

She had rather full lips and her cheek dimpled as she gave him half a smile. "Why don't you call me Laura? I don't want people thinking you're the family chauffeur or something—even if you are."

"All right, Laura. If you call me Bobby."

Her frown was amused. "Must I? It's a little boy's name—or a teen idol from the Fifties." She was teasing but there was meanness behind it. If was as if she couldn't decide whether to flirt with him or insult him.

"It's what my friends call me."

"Is that what you want us to be?" she asked, acidly. "Friends?"

He smiled, but narrowed his eyes. "Are we getting off on the wrong foot?"

She blinked, swallowed, shook her head, no. "I'll . . . I'll do my best not to take it out on you."

Through the portal to the living room, Wynn emerged, in a yellow polo and gray slacks and sock-clad feet; nice to know rich people took their shoes off, at home, like the common folk.

"I see you've met," Wynn said, with a toned-down version of the dazzling smile. He went to his daughter, touched her arm gently. "I hope you're all right with this, dear. . . ."

She gave him a witheringly sarcastic version of her own dazzling smile. "Do I have a choice?"

Wynn laughed nervously. "You're going to give Detective Simone the wrong impression about us, dear."

"We mustn't have that. Impressions are so very important."

Wynn gave her a hurt look that turned firm, or tried to, as he said, "Be good."

She sighed, nodded, and her voice was not at all unkind as she said, "I will, Daddy," and kissed him on the cheek.

In a singsong voice as if to a child, she said, "Come along, Bobby," and went to the door, revealing a rolled-up script shoved in the back pocket of her jeans—also revealing a very nicely shaped, if rather generous, rear end.

"Thank you, Detective Simone," Wynn said, face tight with concern and something else . . . sorrow?

"Don't mention it," Simone said, and followed her out.

The rental car—a sleek dark blue Ford Taurus—was in the underground lot in a guest space near the elevator.

"Pretty nice wheels for a civil servant," she said.

"It's a rental."

"On Daddy? You should've sprung for a Mercedes Benz E-three-twenty."

He opened the rider's side door for her. "Would you rather I had?"

"Hell no." She flounced the blond ponytail as she slipped into the car seat. "I don't like showing off wealth. My friends are in theater, and they're mostly poverty-stricken. Do I look like the kind of person who'd rub that in their faces?"

"Yes."

That froze her smart-ass expression and he shut the door on it.

She sat sullenly while he drove, catching Broadway at Columbus Circle. It was a straight shot to the East Village, a fairly quick ride and traffic was relatively light—it was just after seven, and her rehearsal was at seven-thirty.

About halfway there, she said, "I don't mean to be a bitch."

"I don't mean to be a bastard."

That made her smile a little. "Let's strive for a little honesty here, shall we? I wasn't fooled by this for a second."

He glanced at her. "Fooled by what?"

"That you've been hired to protect me from flash bulbs and *Hard Copy*."

"I think with who your father is, and all the media the trial attracted, it's a valid concern."

She was quite animated, and affected, as she spoke. "Fine, fine, but this is about seeing that I stay off the sauce. You know it, I know it, Daddy knows it . . . let's not kid ourselves. Let's not insult each other's intelligence."

"Okay."

They were stopped at a light. He looked over at her. God, she was a lovely woman; her light blue spooky stunning eyes were fixed on him like pleasant laser beams.

She said, "Just so you know: I've been sober two

months. The very smell of liquor makes me nauseous. I don't like the person I become when I drink, and most people don't like that person, either."

"Sounds like you've got it together."

"I do. I have. I am."

"Good. Good for you."

The light changed; he drove on.

She folded her arms across her generous bosom. "But I resent having a babysitter. I resent what my father's doing to me. It's . . . humiliating."

"Look, he obviously cares. Give it some time. He'll back off. He'll learn to, you know . . . trust you."

Her voice was part whine, part accusation. "I'll tell you how much he trusts me. A year ago, he forced me to move back home."

"Forced you?"

She sat sideways in the seat, to look at him better, yanking the seat-belt strap around to do so. "Hey. I'm a working actor. I never had my father pull any strings for me, I never asked for anything but the chance to make it on my own. Most people in my position wouldn't even bother working. You know, I've been around those kind of people all my life— some of them are three, four, five generations away from where the money started. They're lazy assholes, living off money earned by some hardworking, enterprising ancestor who died before they were born."

Hearing this admission from a rich person was a little surprising, and refreshing. "Don't they usually go into the family business?"

"No. Oh, some of 'em pretend—like my father. But he doesn't do anything, really—except buy artwork and travel and go to board meetings and run in the right circles. *I* wanted to work, to pursue my art, my craft. I come into money in a few years, Bobby—when I turn thirty-five, which in a way is sooner than I want it to be. My trust fund will be handed over to me, and I'll be a millionaire."

"Cool."

"You know, all I ever asked of my parents was a small monthly stipend so I could pay my rent and just nominally exist . . . that's all. A pittance. Probably no more than you make."

"Really." Simone was starting to understand how a rich girl like Laura defined "making it on her own."

"Jesus, I miss my apartment. You know, I used to live over near Jefferson Market—Patchin Place. Little hideaway court . . ."

"Over on West Tenth?"

"Yeah. But Daddy pulled the plug—stopped my monthly allowance and told me if I wanted him to 'underwrite' me any more, I'd have to go into rehab."

"Which you did."

"Yes, which I did! Only when I got out, he made me move back into my old room, like I was sixteen, not twenty-five!"

At that moment, she seemed sixteen, but Simone said, "That's rough."

A grunt of disgust rose from the nice chest. "He says he'll let me know when he feels I'm . . . ready . . . to live on my own, again."

"So, till then, you have to put up with certain indignities . . . like me."

They traded smiles.

"You're not so bad," she said, "as indignities go. You're a good listener. An actor likes a good listener."

They were stopped at a light again.

Her face was washed in red. "At least Daddy does believe in me as an artist. An actor. He always has."

"That counts for something," Simone said. "It's not the most practical profession."

"That's what my mother used to say. And I used to say, who cares if it's practical, we're fucking rich, aren't we?" She giggled, then said, "That got me slapped, a few times. She was as ugly a drunk as I am."

"I'm sorry."

"No, Bobby boy, she wasn't supportive about my acting at all."

"Hadn't she been an actress herself?"

"Yes, and hated it. Used it as a stepping-stone to land somebody rich . . . *Daddy*—though she *was* pretty good. Better than she knew. Ever see 'Holiday in a Goldfish Bowl'?"

"I don't think so."

"It turns up on TV."

"I'll watch for it."

The light turned green and they moved forward.

"Mother wanted me to get married," she said, her throaty voice soft but edged with bitterness, "have children, make another generation of wealthy worthless wimps who never have to work."

"Maybe she just wanted grandchildren." He glanced over at her. "That's normal enough."

Laura turned the blue laser beams on him again and smirked. "She wanted Victoria Wynn's daughter to marry somebody else of 'high standing,' which is a laugh, considering she was from a family of steel workers in Gary, Indiana."

Simone smiled, thinking he didn't mind coming from mean streets, because he'd had loving parents with the common sense to teach him life was leavened with both happiness and sorrow.

"Listen," she said, "you could do me a big favor."

"Try me."

"It'd be an embarrassment to me if my colleagues found out you were my . . . retinue. However they take it, it'll be demeaning. I mean, if they think I have a bodyguard 'cause I'm a rich girl ducking the spotlight, or especially if they figure out Daddy's watching to see if I . . . tumble off a bar stool. . . ."

Simone's head moved back and forth in a "don't worry about it" gesture. "You just tell me what you want me to say."

She was studying him. "I'm not seeing anybody right now, so . . . you could be my boyfriend. You're not entirely stupid."

"Thanks."

"You got a look. Distinctive look. Puerto Rican?"

"French-Portuguese."

"That's an interesting cocktail."

He looked at her, smiled. A little. "You don't touch cocktails anymore, remember?"

"Good point." She had great teeth; he wondered if God gave them to her, or Daddy. "So—you want to be my guy? You don't have to pretend to be affectionate or anything. I'm not real touchy feely, unlike most actors. So nobody'll think it's weird, us not hanging on to each other or anything."

"I'm up for it," he said. "Just don't ask me to give a fake name or anything."

She shook her head. "No, you can be who are you. Bobby Simone. Cute cop."

Now all of a sudden, *he* was an actor! He felt a twinge of panic. "What if somebody asks how we met?"

"Nobody'll ask. They'll just assume it's because of what happened to my mother. There were a lot of cops in my family's life, for a while there."

Just below Union Square Park, the Marian Wald Theater—an old neighborhood movie house, converted over twenty years ago and named for the famous actress—was on East 13th between University Place and Fifth Avenue. Simone dropped Laura off at the theater, watched her go safely in, then found a parking place on the street; this was very much his turf as a cop, an area that was still seedy but gradually gentrifying, with streets that gathered an eclectic mix of citizenry—drug addicts and Yuppies, college students and street people.

He found his way into the theater, which had been remodeled very little since its movie-house days; the substitution of handcrafted posters for movie one-sheets and a concession stand that omitted popcorn and added cappuccino were about it. The place was clean enough but charmingly long in the tooth, and the original art-deco moldings and fixtures seemed apropos for a theater that specialized in reviving for-gotten plays of the 30s and 40s.

Onstage, a run-through had begun—just begun, he soon realized—and he settled into a seat about a third of the way from the back. The seats were un-padded wooden ones that had apparently been here since at least the 40s, and—long-legged as he was—he had trouble getting comfortable.

Up front, here and there, actors who weren't on-stage at the moment sat, watching, waiting. A man and a woman sat in the fourth row, and Simone had a hunch one of them was the director, the other an assistant, but couldn't guess which was which.

Laura was onstage with two actors, one hunkily handsome in a conventional soap-opera lead kind of way, the other pleasant-looking and pudgy and try-ing a little too hard to be funny. The set was simple—a table and a few other sticks of secondhand-store furniture, a slightly expressionistic flat suggesting a dining room, in what Simone guessed was supposed to be the 1930s or early 40s. It wasn't a dress re-hearsal, so Laura's black jeans and turtleneck, and the jeans and sweatshirts of the two male actors, didn't exactly convey the period.

The play seemed to be realistic at first—Laura was the wife, the handsome actor was her husband, and the pudgy actor was a freeloading friend who lived with them; they were supposed to be in late middle-age, and both men worked in a factory. Laura played a complaining wife, though the husband deserved the shit he was getting. It became clear that the hus-band had invented various things the factory was manufacturing but had allowed himself to be taken advantage of by the boss.

Turned out it was a fantasy, with the inventor husband building a time machine to take him and his dim-witted friend back to when they were young men, to change their lives. Laura was very winning, playing the wife when she was the inventor's young sweetheart, and it was charming and poignant, because the inventor falls in love with her all over again, but forces himself to marry the boss's daughter instead.

Then it jumped to the point in time where the play began, only now the inventor is an unhappy rich co-partner in the factory. Realizing this life wasn't really as good as what he'd had, the inventor and his pal ("Whatever happened to that machine we used to have?") go back in time, and put everything back the way it was. Laura, as the complaining wife, remembers her alternate life (where she'd married somebody rich herself) as a bad dream, and realizes she's happier this way. But the inventor husband has learned not be such a sap and improves their lives by standing up to the boss.

Simone enjoyed it; it was wordy and kind of corny, but the actors were pretty good (particularly Laura, who was much less animated and affected onstage than in real life), and the simple sets gave it a dream-like feeling. At the end of each act (there were three), the actors took a break while the director (turned out it was the woman) gave them notes on their performances. Simone felt smug when the director told the pudgy guy to quit trying to be funny.

By 11 p.m. it was over, and Laura came back to where Simone was sitting and scooted in next to him.

"So what did you think?"

"I enjoyed it."

She liked hearing that. "Kinda sweet, isn't it? Wouldn't it be nice to have a machine like that? Where you could go back and improve things? Do things different? Or not do them at all?"

"But at the end they put things back the way they were."

"Improved, though," she said. "They do improve their lives. Do I seem too bitchy?"

"No! If I was the wife, I woulda *left* the creep, not just ragged him."

"Me too," she laughed. "Listen, it's kind of a tradition, after rehearsal, some of us go over to the Coffee Shop."

"I know the place."

"Come along and, you know . . . be my boyfriend."

"My pleasure."

Coffee Shop, on the corner of 16th and Union Square, was larger than its name implied, though it did serve diner-style food and had been around long enough to be legitimately 50s retro. With lighting far dimmer than your typical coffee shop, Coffee Shop also served liquor. In the bar area, at a table, five actors and one off-duty detective were crowded around.

They were all smoking, except for Simone; and they were all drinking, except for Simone and Laura. Mostly it was beer, but Guy Hamilton—the handsome actor, whose significant other was Laurence

Philborn, the pudgy actor—was knocking back bourbon and Coke like it was just Coke.

"*You're* a real person," Guy said to Simone, who'd been accepted by one and all as Laura's fella. "What do *you* think of this piece of shit?"

"What piece of shit?" Simone asked.

"This play. This justifiably forgotten tidbit of 1930s trivia. 'It's a Wonderful Life Meets Back to the Future.' "

"I like it."

"Why?"

"I don't know. It's just kind of entertaining. You guys are doin' a nice job with it."

"Thank you," Laurence Philborn said.

Eyes crinkling devilishly, Laura asked, "Why are *you* in this 'piece of shit,' Guy, if you hate it so much?"

Guy said, "Because it's so much better than the shit that pays," and drained his latest bourbon and Coke.

Later, in the car, on their way up Broadway, Laura said, "Guy's a soap-opera actor."

Simone smiled, feeling smug again.

"That's why we're rehearsing at night," she said. "Around his schedule."

"He's pretty good. Not as good as you are."

"Thanks. He's sort of a name, for us. He'll draw us some busloads of ladies with blue hair . . . and maybe we'll get to extend our run."

Simone glanced at her. "Can I ask you something?"

"Sure."

"Why put yourself through that?"

'Through what?"

"Being around it. Around drinking."

Her expression was patient, as if she were dealing with a slow but lovable child. "Bobby—it's part of the life. Theater is very social. Part of it is unwinding afterward, with your friends, your peers. And I'm one of the leads. It would be rude if I didn't go out with them, at least part of the time."

"Does it bother you, sitting there while other people drink?"

"No. Except, like I told you—the smell. Makes me sick."

"Doesn't it make you want have a drink?"

"No."

He wondered if she was telling the truth. And if she was lying, was it to him, or herself?

Before long, he was pulling into the underground parking garage for her building, and easing the rental Ford into one of the guest stalls.

He shut the car off. "You want me to walk you up?"

She gave him the dazzling Wynn smile. "This really is like a date, isn't it, Bobby? No. No thanks."

"Same time tomorrow night?"

She let out a small, throaty laugh. "My, this *is* getting serious. I haven't gone out with a boy named 'Bobby' since I was in high school. . . . You think I was bitchy?"

"No, I told you, the husband deserved it, he—"

"I didn't mean in the play. I meant, earlier. When you picked me up."

"No. Well. Maybe a little."

She was sitting sideways on the seat again, but with the seat belt off. "It wasn't you. It was Daddy I was mad at. But I guess I should thank him."

"Why?"

She leaned over and kissed Simone, gently, on the mouth.

" 'Cause if I have to have an escort," she said, still very close to him, "I want it to be a big tall handsome French-Portuguese cop who likes corny plays . . . and me in them."

Then she kissed him again, not so gently, and he felt himself kissing her back, then drew away.

"I . . . I don't know," he said. "I'm getting paid to look out for you."

"I'm not drinking, am I?" she said, and kissed him again. He put his arms around her, drew her to him. High school kids making out in a car. . . .

She whispered in his ear: "And it's all right that you're getting paid . . . you're not a whore. Just an actor . . . playing my boyfriend."

Then she slipped out of the rider's side and her nice full behind in the tight black jeans twitched its way to the elevator and she was gone.

The scent of her perfume was lingering in the car, or anyway in his nostrils; very pleasant—and familiar.

Then he recognized it, and he felt suddenly guilty, and his erection shriveled.

Bijan.

Diane's perfume.

SEVEN

Detective Third Grade Diane Russell was thrilled to be back on days, but two weeks ago, had Lt. Fancy made the suggestion, she'd have somehow wormed her way out. She would not have wanted to be around her friends on the Day Tour—in particular, Bobby—because she knew she wasn't over the hump.

Night Tour, they didn't know her, except for Greg, who was aware of what she was going through and helped cover for her. The early weeks had been brutal—her skin crawling, shakes so bad she could barely write legibly; it was all she could do to raise a coffee cup to her lips without spilling. When they were out on the street, it wasn't as bad, the night air felt good, she was just another anonymous soul in the city; but at her desk, where she was a specific person under the eyes of others, she felt terribly uncomfortable. She could sit still, but not very.

And at home, in her apartment, despite the room-darkening window shades she'd bought, sleeping during the day had been next to impossible. Andy said that had nothing to do with working Night Tour, though; he said insomnia was par for the course. When you dried out on your own, when you didn't check yourself in somewhere and get help, you had your work cut out for you. So Andy said.

And he would know.

These last two weeks, however, all of that had begun gradually turning around. She was sleeping well. Eating better. The trembling was intermittent, now, and not nearly so severe (if Fancy had known how bad her shakes were, he wouldn't have let her wear a gun on her hip). She felt good, and there was sublime pleasure in that, and in the simple joy of a good night's sleep.

And when she was awake, she was no longer measuring time in the segments between drinks. There was a new, and wonderful, open-endedness to her sense of time.

But Russell wasn't absolutely sure she was over the hump, even now; she still, periodically, all too frequently, had the craving. Stress could kick it in, emotional turmoil . . . ironically, seeing Bobby, and craving him, made her crave *it*. Fortunately, when she was actually around the stuff, the smell of it made her sick, and that helped keep it from her lips.

Not that she had been around it that much—in her personal life, she avoided the old haunts, not just bars but restaurants that served liquor (as Andy put it, "You gotta stay off slippery territory—them old playmates, old playgrounds"). Yet as a detective out on the streets, you sometimes had to go into a bar to question somebody. Or you might go into somebody's residence to question them and find them nursing a drink.

Like right now.

She and Greg Medavoy were in a living room that was spacious and sun-flooded and hospital-room stark, its off-white walls hung sparingly with yellow-and-green abstract tempera paintings that looked like particularly inspired kindergarten work. The geometric shapes of vintage 50s furnishings—kidney-shaped glass coffee table, rust-color boomerang chair, square white couch with square overstuffed pillows, nubby green easy chair with wooden-dowel legs, skinny metal round-shaded floor lamp—were precisely positioned on a square of carpet (tan and gray squares alternating) of a man-made fiber that last week would have been considered gauche. In this well-designed retro-modern world, Russell (in her olive polo and tan khakis) and Greg (in his brown suit with yellow and brown tie) were rumpled, drab, postmodern aberrations.

They were definitely off their beat, this morning; this penthouse, in an apartment building that dated to the 20s, was in the trendy Chelsea district. Its occupant, Constance Reed, sister of the late Victoria Wynn, sat in the boomerang chair with a big white cat on the lap of her white ski pants, which matched her white turtleneck; she was nursing a Scotch on the rocks which she'd acquired from a small bar in one corner of the room, a wrought-iron affair with an abstract-shape masonite countertop.

The detectives were on the couch, where their hostess had bid them sit, and Russell considered putting her sunglasses back on, that was how bright the afternoon sun was, even filtered through the sheer white drapes.

Constance Reed was a slender, even skinny woman, rather tall, in her late forties; her dark brown hair was fairly short, sleek and perfect, framing her well-carved features in twin arcs. She wore too much makeup, in that drag queen manner some older actresses unwittingly affected; but she remained strikingly beautiful, in a plastic surgery–maintained fashion-model manner at odds with the more all-American look of her late sister, Victoria Wynn. Her long narrow legs were crossed in an X, as she brought a Gwen Verdon–ish grace to sitting in a chair that was nearly impossible to sit gracefully in.

Both detectives knew quite a bit about Constance Reed; there were many questions they need not ask, having pooled their tabloid-nourished knowledge on the way over in the unmarked car.

Greg, driving, had asked, "They weren't twins, were they?"

"No," Russell had said. "Two years apart. But there is, or anyway was, a strong resemblance."

"Regular Betty and Veronica," Greg said, perhaps a little starstruck about going to visit a celebrity of sorts. "Midwest girls, and they both become actresses . . . movie stars."

"Well, they were both in movies," Russell said, considerably less impressed. "Connie was a Vegas showgirl for a while, you know."

Greg nodded. "Yeah, I read that. You know who she dated, don't you?"

"Yeah. I plan to bring that up—but not right away."

He grinned. "Good move, Diane."

The Landon sisters had been local beauty queens back home in Gary, Indiana, and Connie had followed Vicki to Hollywood, where the older sister had had some success with supporting roles in theatrical features and starring ones on TV. But Connie—though just as pretty as her sister, and easily more talented, with a strong dance background—hadn't done as well as Vicki in Tinsel Town. The younger Landon had landed only a few B movie roles—drive-in stuff, beach party and hell's angels movies—before taking her terpsichorean talents, and slenderly shapely figure, to Vegas.

Marriage to wealthy J. Michael turned minor movie actress Vicki Landon into social butterfly Victoria Wynn, and her sister followed a few years later, wedding a high-ranking executive in one of the Wynn family's insurance companies. Soon the sisters (with their husbands) were society-page regulars.

Socialite Constance Reed was much more famous than B-movie starlet/Vegas showgirl Connie Landon had ever been, and in the late 70s, she had used her jet-set–ish fame to get back into acting. She landed a few made-for-TV movies, did some off-Broadway in New York, appeared on "Hollywood Squares" and well into the mid-1980s traveled with road companies of Broadway shows, musicals and Neil Simon, mostly. There were those who considered her a campy joke—her ex-husband among them—but Russell had seen Constance Reed in an all-star revival of

The Front Page at Lincoln Center, and thought she was pretty good.

All of these facts were fixed in the minds of both detectives because the Victoria Wynn murder—and all of the players in that real-life melodrama—had been the subject of more press than the moon landing, and subject to wider-spread speculation than "who killed JR."

"If you don't m-mind," Greg said, placing a small silver tape recorder on the glass coffee-table top, "we would like to record this conversation, and also take a few notes."

"I have tried, since day one, to be cooperative," Constance Reed said, her pitch low, her manner theatrical, nodding assent to Greg's request, stroking her white cat with a pale slender hand whose nails were painted blood-red, loose gold bracelets clinking. "But I fail to understand why we must go over this ground yet again."

Notepad and pencil in hand, Greg sat forward and his upper lip pulled back over his teeth in that grimace of a nervous smile of his. "Well, we . . . we're n-n-new to this case, Mrs. Reed. We need the background to be properly informed."

She arched an already arching, penciled-on eyebrow. "Every sentient citizen in this city and most people with a pulse in America know the details of this case."

"Mrs. Reed," Russell said, her own notebook and pen in hand, "we're not investigating your sister's murder, not directly."

"I know," she said imperiously, petting the cat.

"You're looking into that"—the next word came out as if obscene—"prosecutor's apartment getting broken into. . . . Michael called me and told me, after you spoke to him."

Russell and Greg exchanged a quick glance, then Russell continued with the questioning. "You and your brother-in-law are pretty tight."

"Yes we are." There was a cool defiance to her responses; Russell jotted down *defensive, condescending*. "Michael and I have been good friends for a very long time."

"Would you say," Russell went on, "that you were closer to him than with your sister?"

She sipped her Scotch, the ice, the glass, glinting from the sunlight. "My sister and I had problems. We didn't view the world the same way. . . . Victoria used show business as a stepping-stone to marrying money . . . and achieving social standing."

Whereas you married money and used your social standing to get back into show business, Russell thought.

"If you could just please h-humor us," Greg said, giving her his affable but ill-at-ease smile, "just briefly going over the events of the night of your sister's murder. . . ."

Constance Reed sighed so heavily it disturbed the cat, which jumped onto the floor and scurried away. "Michael came over about seven," she said. "As you well know, the doorman of the building saw him come in. We talked about some private family matters—"

Russell asked, "What were those private family matters?"

The nature of those "family matters" had not come out in court, due to a ruling on a lack of relevance.

She shook her head regally, hair shimmering. "My niece and I have been very close. She's an actress, too, you know, and I suppose I've been something of a . . . mentor . . . perhaps a role model to the child. I never had children of my own, and . . . her mother didn't encourage her in her theatrical interests, in fact quite the opposite."

Russell's eyes tightened. "And that's what you and Mr. Wynn discussed, all night?"

She shook her head, no, and the perfect arcs of brunette hair swung; was that a wig? "Laura . . . Laura has a drinking problem. And at that point in time, she wasn't recognizing it. But her father wanted to get her some help. He had a plan to cut off her allowance and essentially force her into rehabilitation. *That's* what we discussed."

Greg asked, "And, uh . . . how did her mother feel about that?"

"Victoria was an alcoholic, also. She denied it in herself, and in her daughter. She felt the major problem in Laura's life was that Laura was following in my footsteps, not hers."

Russell sat forward. "What do you mean?"

A faint sneer formed on the overly lipsticked mouth. "Victoria wanted only the best for her daughter—which to my sister meant her daughter marrying money, as if the Wynns didn't already have enough. But it was more a class thing, you understand." The sneer turned less faint. "Show business, after all, was for 'carnival people.' "

Russell asked, "Where was Laura in the midst of this discussion that pertained to her?"

"Upstate, in the mountains, with her boyfriend, at the family cabin."

Russell figured the Wynn family "cabin" was probably three floors with crystal chandeliers.

"Surely," Constance Reed continued, "*that's* in your records."

Greg touched his chest with his notebook and seemed apologetic as he said, "We have to ask these questions ourselves, Mrs. Reed. We have to develop our own perspective, so to speak."

Constance Reed rolled her eyes, drained the last of her double shot of Scotch on the rocks, rose, unfolding from the low-slung chair with the elegance of a blooming rose as caught by slow-motion photography. She glided to the boomerang bar and mixed another.

Russell said, "Your brother-in-law stayed the night with you."

She nodded, matter-of-factly, moving with catlike grace back to sitting area, going to the nubby chair this time, which put her closer to Russell. "Michael and Victoria had been fighting. He had just suggested to her that both she and Laura needed to go into rehab."

"Your sister could be violent. . . ."

She shrugged, fluttered eyelashes God hadn't given her. "Vicki had a vile temper. But I loved my sister, please understand. I just didn't happen to like her. Also, understand, when she was not drinking she could be incredibly charming."

Greg said, "Mr. Wynn was here, with you, when your sister's body was discovered."

Russell could smell the Scotch; it sickened her, yet stirred something.

"Yes," Constance Reed was saying, "George found the body when he arrived for work in the morning."

Greg looked up from his notebook. "George?"

"Their butler. He'd had the previous evening off. When he left, just after seven p.m., my sister was still alive. When he arrived for work the next morning, at six-thirty a.m., he found her dead in the kitchen. Michael was still here with me when you people called about Victoria's death. You know all this. Why belabor—"

Russell asked, "Was it typical of your brother-in-law to stay the night?"

She sighed, sipped the drink, gestured expansively with the glass in hand; its fragrance wafted under Russell's nostrils like a sickening perfume. "When Victoria was a raging, abusive harridan, yes I have a convertible sofa in the guest room. Michael and I share a love and concern for Laura . . . we talked deep into the night about the need to get her into Betty Ford. We also, that night, both decided that Victoria was a lost cause."

Russell allowed a tiny smirk to dig into her cheek. "I guess you were right."

"That's a little catty, isn't it, detective? A little cruel?" Another sip—actually, more a gulp; the ice clinked. Russell felt nauseated.

"Yes it was," Russell said. "Sorry."

"Whether Michael and I are friends with a mutual

caring interest in his daughter . . . as I've indicated . . . or if my brother-in-law and I were, as the media has slanderously speculated, lovers, the facts remain unchanged: Michael spent the night here."

And Constance Reed had been Michael's unshakable alibi throughout the trial—the single major reason (jurors told the media, later) that he'd gotten off. The fact that the doorman of Mrs. Reed's building had seen Wynn come in but not go out meant little: there was a back way out. It would have been easy enough for Wynn to slip out, commit the crime, and return.

"Mrs. Reed," Russell said, looking at her notebook, "you worked in Las Vegas for several years."

"As a dancer, yes. For just under three years. I was a featured performer."

"At the Riviera," Russell said.

"Yes. And the Flamingo."

"You were friendly with a Frankie Dellacroce."

". . . Frank and I were friendly, yes."

"You dated him."

"We went out a few times."

"You had a relationship with Frank Dellacroce."

"We were friendly."

"Mrs. Reed, were you aware that Mr. Dellacroce was a New York mobster with Nevada business interests?"

"I was young, he had show business connections, he was good looking, he was well spoken, he wore beautiful clothes. Any other questions about my 'relationship' with Frank?"

She sighed disgustedly, and sipped the Scotch.

Russell said, "He's been in Sing Sing since '91."

"I read the papers."

"Extortion charges. Conspiracy. Assault."

"I haven't spoken to Frank since Vegas. I was a naive young woman . . ."

Russell had her doubts about whether Constance Reed had ever been a naive young woman.

". . . who had a 'relationship' with an attractive man she thought might help her career. Why are you bringing this up, in this context?"

Greg twitched his nervous smile again and said, "Ma'am, we have reason to believe that the perpetrator-type individuals who broke into the Sipowicz apartment were professionals."

"Professional *killers*," Russell elaborated. "The sort of men a man like Frank Dellacroce could access."

There was outrage in the woman's frozen smile and furrowed brow. "And you think because I once dated Frank, I could access those kind of people? That if I could, I would? Are you accusing me of something?"

Greg patted the air with a palm, his expression appeasing. "Not at all, Mrs. Reed. We're just examining the facts and parties involved. . . ."

Constance Reed set down her glass of Scotch so hard the glass coffee-table top might have shattered; Greg's little silver tape recorder jumped. She stood, chin raised, eyes slitted.

"This little interview is over," she said, and pointed grandly to the door.

In the car, as he drove, Greg said, "You know,

Diane, nobody ever came up with any evidence that she and Wynn were lovers. And you gotta think the media gave it the old college try."

"I know. But rich people know how to be discreet. Besides, she used to be Frankie the Snake's girlfriend; she knows how to sneak around."

Greg's grin was much more at ease, now. "She sure didn't like you bringing *that* up."

"No. But let's say the theory Sylvia floated in court, that Constance Reed was Wynn's accomplice, and that Wynn sneaked in and out of her building, to do the deed—"

"A theory Sylvia never got past the judge," Greg reminded her, "on grounds of insubstantiation."

"—so okay, let's say that theory is incorrect. Let's say Wynn really did spend the night with his sister-in-law, and whether they were in the sack or not doesn't matter, does it? Not if Victoria Wynn was the victim of a professional killer, herself."

Greg winced. "But she was slashed to death with a kitchen knife. It looked like a crime of passion . . . a vicious one, at that."

Russell nodded. "Yes, but our contract-killer at large, Leonard Parsons, has an M.O. of making his murders look like home invasions got-out-of-hand. Leaving Victoria Wynn dead on the floor, killed with a kitchen knife, is consistent with that."

"There were no signs of forced entry—"

"It still could easily have been viewed as a sophisticated home invasion gone awry—Victoria Wynn interrupted the thief and got killed for her trouble."

"Well—"

"Maybe that's how it was *supposed* to look . . . and if you remember, that notion came up, early on in the investigation, first day or two."

Greg was nodding, remembering. "Only with the reports of violent arguments between husband and wife, and the blood found at the scene with DNA matching Wynn's, that home invasion theory never got seriously floated, after that."

They stopped at a light.

Greg had a thoughtful expression as he looked over at her and asked, "What do you think, Diane? Were they lovers, J. Michael Wynn and Constance, back there?"

"I'm not sure," she shrugged. "You never know, with love."

"Tell me about it."

"But I do know one thing."

"What?"

"Connie knocks the sauce back pretty good," Russell said, "for somebody counseling her niece about getting into rehab."

EIGHT

It came as something of a surprise to Andy Sipowicz—plowing through the records that were the official memories of his working life—how few enemies he had. He wasn't sure, in this instance, whether to be pleasantly surprised or disappointed.

First of all, a lot of the perps with reason to hate him were still inside, warming cells at Riker's, Sing Sing, and other fine New York state correctional facilities.

Second of all, these incarcerated individuals—like that bastard who beat his wife to death last year, or that scumbag who raped and killed that little boy, year before that—were not the type who would likely inspire the sort of devotion and sense of obligation that might arouse thoughts of vengeance in friends and/or family.

Take those punks that kidnapped that pregnant black girl and raped her and killed her and burned her body, a few months ago. Would even their white-trash tribe harbor thoughts of getting back at the asshole cop who had the gall to remove such prime examples of human achievement off the city streets?

Anyway, most of the sterling citizens Sipowicz had sent away were too far down the food chain to be likely candidates for hiring professional assassins; gang members, drug addicts, pimps and armed robbers, these types tended to do their own dirty work or at least find a similarly twisted acquaintance to do it for them.

He did figure there was one lead worth checking out, an obvious one but definitely involved a class of individual that had the financial wherewithal—and the proper, or maybe that was improper, connections—to hire the likes of Leonard Parsons and his as-yet-nameless hawk-faced associate.

Bobby was off checking out a couple of weak leads generated by his scouring of Sylvia's cases, so Sipowicz went over to the desk of Detective James Martinez, who was filling out a DD-5, to invite him along.

"I could use a little back-up on an excursion into lasagna land," Sipowicz said. "You got any pressing engagements?"

Not surprisingly, James was game. Bright-eyed, eager, James had come downstairs from Anti-Crime to do a few fill-in jobs, notably when Sipowicz was off the job healing up from Alfonse Giardella shooting him. So impressed was the Loo with James's hard work and dogged persistence, not to mention cheerful fucking attitude, the kid got invited to that unending party that was life at the 15th squad, earning his gold shield in record time. Of course, being Hispanic hadn't hurt the kid in that regard, Sipowicz knew, but James was good people.

"Adrianne can beep me, if we catch anything,"

James said, getting up, glancing over at Detective Lesniak at her desk nearby, who overheard and waved her assent.

Sipowicz said, "Bring along one of them circulars they worked up."

The mug shot of Leonard Parsons and the police sketch of his accomplice were part of a "Have you seen these men?" circular that had been sent out to restaurants and hotels in the city.

"Sure thing," James said, and went into Interview One, where a stack of the circulars was on the counter.

As they passed Miss Abandando's desk, and her shrine to the New York Rangers, Sipowicz said, "Tell Detective Simone, when he gets back in, I went out on a fact-findin' mission."

The carefully coiffed blonde Miss Abandando, bedecked in a light blue spangly pants suit that Sipowicz figured would've looked just peachy on stage at the Grand Ole Opry, nodded, and asked, "And if the lieutenant inquires about your whereabouts?"

"You can tell him the same thing. Do I look like a guy with somethin' to hide?"

"Not at all, Detective," she said, quiet amusement tickling that cute apple-cheeked kisser.

"Probably shootin' blanks with this trip," Sipowicz said, as he and James headed down the stairs, "but I keep this ass duty up, I'm gonna lose my robust tan."

James was wearing an elaborate shoulder rig for his automatic, his green tie flapping on his dark green plaid shirt. *What, does this kid dress in the dark?*

Sipowicz wondered, his own red and green tie neatly clasped to his blue-checked shirt.

"Where we headed, Detective?"

"Look, kid, you got your shield, you're in the club, it's 'Andy,' all right? No formalities."

"Sure, Andy. Why don't you call me 'James,' then."

"James, we're headin' to someplace I took you once before."

"Oh, yeah." A grin formed under the trim mustache. "I think I know."

"Sure you do, kid. You're a detective."

They were downstairs now, moving past desk sergeant Agostini, though the bustle of uniforms, detectives, clerks, and civilians that made the 15th Precinct what it was—to James Martinez, an exciting array of human problems waiting to be solved, to Andy Sipowicz, the refuse can of society, waiting to be emptied.

In the unmarked car, which Sipowicz drove, James inquired about how Sylvia was doing.

"She says it don't bother her," Sipowicz said, caught behind a UPS truck. "I mean, why should she be bothered, couple guys come in, shoot the place up, probably meanin' to kill one or both of us. That's pretty much an everyday occurrence, right, in the life of us boys in blue?"

James winced in sympathy. "You think she's, like, repressing or suppressing it or whatever?"

"Not exactly. These days, I go to lay a loaf, I got multiple choice on the new assholes she tore me lately."

James smirked humorlessly, shaking his head. "Takin' it out on you, huh? Tough—on both of ya. It's gotta be wearin' on her. Her mind's gotta be turnin' this over and over. If those guys were what you think they are . . . I mean, if we're talkin' hit men, here . . . they're still *out* there."

That had been the topic of their latest fight. Last night Sipowicz had tried to get Sylvia to take a leave of absence from the District Attorney's office, and go hide out with one of her out-of-town relatives, of which she had plenty. There were Greeks all up and down the Eastern Seaboard she could shack with till the heat died down.

"Andy," she said, sitting at her computer in the nook of the living room that served as her at-home office, "we're safe here. They're not coming back."

Sipowicz was feeding his fish. "How do you know that? You say that with such certainty. All of a sudden, you're psychic?"

She sighed, and it was clear her patience was running thin. "Wasn't it you who wanted me to take a leave of absence and stay home, the other day? You said it yourself—they're not coming back because they screwed up. They're not coming back, not when there's a cop with a gun waiting for them."

Sipowicz was shaking his head, no. "They wait a few days, let us get our guard down, these types, they're military types. Like commandos, any second, they can storm the place."

"I would think they'd have left town by now."

"Not till they finish what they was hired to do."

"Now *you're* the psychic one."

He put down the box of fish food and went over to her, looming over her as she sat in the glow of the monitor.

"Okay," he said, "say you're right. Say Leonard Parsons and his pal with the hook nose, they're back in Chicago splittin' a deep dish pizza, right about now. That just means whoever hired 'em is siccin' somebody new on us."

"Are you trying to scare me, Andy?"

"Hell, yes, I'm tryin' to scare ya!" He began to pace. "I want you to disappear till this is over. That plaster work over there, that smell of paint in the air, that's covering up bullet holes in our freakin' wall, Sylvia."

Her expression was weary as she began to say, "Andy—"

And the phone rang.

"I better get it," he said.

She nodded glumly.

He went to it, and it was Diane Russell. He talked to her for about five minutes and when he came back, Sylvia was sitting on the couch with her arms folded and her eyes narrowed and her jaw firm.

"Your friend again?" she asked.

"Yeah."

"That's the fourth time in two days she's called."

"She and Medavoy are workin' the case; she's keepin' me filled in."

"At home?"

He shrugged. "She probably thinks it's better Fancy don't know she's workin' so close with me on

this. I'm supposed to be off the case except for bein'
a witness."

"*How* close is she working with you, Andy?"

He rolled his eyes, shook his head. "Aw, Sylvia,
you can't be serious. You know I love you, baby."

"I know you do, Andy."

"Why would I want anybody but you? How could
I be luckier than this?"

She touched his arm, and her eyes were sadder
than a clown painting. "It's not so much that I'm
jealous, not in that way . . . but it hurts me to see
you that close to somebody else . . . yes, particularly
a woman. That there's things you share with somebody else that don't share with me."

"You know cops . . . they're asshole buddies."

She arched an eyebrow. "Well, your asshole buddy
has a particularly nice ass."

He threw a hand up. "You finally seen through
me. I admit it. I hired them guys to come in and
shoot holes in the wall so I could trick you into leavin' town to be with a policewoman about half my
age into fat bald middle-aged guys, hey, it's been a
good two, three months since we got married, and I
yearn to spice up my sex life with some variety."

She stood, her eyes wet. "You don't have to be
cruel."

"Look . . . baby . . ."

Her smile was a thin bitter line. "You know, I think
you're right. Those men might burst in the door any
second now. So stand guard, Andy, okay? You and
your gun sleep out here on the couch, so you can
protect me. And your fish."

The next morning, over a toast-and-coffee breakfast at the kitchen table, he apologized to her.

"It's makin' me crazy," he said, "Fancy keepin' my ass behind a desk like this."

"You know he's doing the right thing," she said. "You know policy doesn't allow cops to work cases that personally involve them."

"Yeah, but between that, and knowin' those two guys're still out there . . ."

"If they're still in the city."

He gestured with his half-eaten slice of toast. "Either way, that Wynn bastard's sittin' eatin' caviar in his Central Park penthouse, gettin' away with his wife's murder."

"We don't know for sure he's the one behind this."

"How can you say that, Sylvia? I heard you say he's an evil sick son of a bitch . . . that him walking was a worse travesty of justice than freakin' O.J. . . ."

"That still doesn't necessarily make him responsible for what happened to us."

Through a bite of toast that he was chewing viciously, Andy growled, "I'd like to go up to that ivory tower of his and have a little private conference with J. Michael Pus-Pimple, and make my own mind up about that."

Her expression was grave. "Don't do it, Andy. You could be throwing your career away."

"Sylvia, I gotta get in the game. I just got to. This sittin' on the bench just ain't cuttin' it."

She reached across the table and touched his hand, gently. "You just don't know for sure he's behind this. Don't go off half-cocked with Wynn, Andy. Promise me."

"Oh, don't worry, baby. I'll be fully cocked."

In Little Italy, ancient tenements decorated with exoskeleton fire escapes, colorful canvas awnings, and vertical neon restaurant signs stared at each other across narrow streets with bumper-to-bumper parking on either side. The cafés and bakeries with their canopied streetside tables were doing a brisk business (when wasn't a good time to stop for a cappuccino?), a reminder that, today, the main allure of that notorious corridor between Mott and Mulberry Street, centering on the blocks around Grand and Hester, was food.

Only a few thousand Italians lived in the district now, most of them in the food service industry; of course, this one time home of the Mafia did maintain its criminal tradition in at least one sense: most of the prices in the restaurants, were highway robbery.

But then, Little Italy had always been about food, hadn't it? Hadn't Joey Gallo been enjoying a seafood dinner at Umberto's Clam House, corner of Mulberry and Hester, when he was shot in 1972? Hadn't Joseph "Butch" Corrao, reputed Gambino capo, once owned the Cafe Biondo? Wasn't Benito's II Restaurant the site of the shooting of Salvatore "Sally Bugs" Briguglio, suspect in the Hoffa disappearance? Wasn't the Ravenite Social Club the favorite hangout of such Little Italy favorite sons as Lucky Luciano, Carlo Gambino, and John Gotti?

And hadn't Minetta's Ristorante Italiano on Mott

Street been home to its owner, Alfonse Giardella, the Merino family's pornography king? Alfonse hadn't died over a plate of clams, but room service of a sort had been delivered to him in the room at the Hotel Saville where he was sequestered, awaiting his opportunity to testify against his former associates.

Sipowicz, with James Martinez following, walked into the unpretentious brick-facade restaurant, leaving a cool sunny afternoon behind, entering the warmth of subdued lighting and dark paneling that was Minetta's. The interior was unpretentious, too, but well-maintained, even if the photos of Italian-American celebrities hanging on the walls, in the bar area up front left, were a little crooked.

The bartender, a bull-necked bucket-headed goombah in a black vest with a black necktie, was washing glasses behind the counter; he had no customers, at the moment. He had worked here a long time, and had seen Sipowicz before.

In fact, Sipowicz had pulled a pre–gold shield James Martinez along for one of his more fabled encounters with Alfonse Giardella within these walls— which included Sipowicz tossing Alfonse's wig across the room like a hairy frisbee.

"Kitchen's closed till four," the bartender said. If his eyes had been narrowed any further, they'd have been shut.

"Don't worry about it," Sipowicz said, waving the guy off, as James followed him deeper into the recesses of the restaurant.

For many years, on weekdays, Alfonse Giardella had held court here, in a rear booth, bookended by bodyguards; after lunch, for several hours (while the restaurant was closed between lunch and dinner), he would do business, take meetings, generally use the booth—as an office. According to Waddell with the Organized Crime Task Force, Angelo Giardella—the heir to Alfonse's smut throne—was maintaining that tradition, at least a few days a week.

Sipowicz, with James in tow, had come down here on the chance that today was one of those days.

And it was, at least if this fashion-model handsome dark-eyed young man sitting alone in Giardella's favorite booth—with not a bodyguard in sight—was Angelo Giardella.

Probably no older than Martinez, he wore a charcoal chalk-striped suit with an eggplant-purple shirt and a charcoal silk tie—an outfit that probably didn't cost any more than a Honda Civic—and his dark hair was moussed back, not pomaded. His eyeglasses were gold, round wireframes. Any remains of lunch had long since been cleared from the linen tablecloth, on which rested only two items: a cellular phone and a folded-over *Wall Street Journal.* He was examining a sheaf of computer printouts, making notations with a silver pen.

He looked up from his work and his expression was pleasantly businesslike as he said, "You gentlemen have the look of authority."

"Underpaid authority," Sipowicz said. "But, yeah, I'd say that's a 'bingo.' Would you be Angelo Giardella?"

"I would." He laid the computer printouts down and touched his cellular phone, lightly. "Is this going to be a conversation we can conduct here, or do I need to contact my attorney?"

"Why don't we just chat awhile, and then you can decide. . . . I'm Detective Sipowicz. This is Detective James Martinez."

A glimmer of recognition registered in the young Giardella's eyes at Sipowicz's name—close-set eyes that were about the only family resemblance to Alfonse that Sipowicz could detect. "Would you like to sit down, detectives?"

"Sure, why not," Sipowicz said, while James pulled a couple chairs over from a nearby table.

"I know who you are, of course," Angelo Giardella said to Sipowicz, removing the wireframe glasses and setting them on the stack of printouts. "I have to admit I'm a little embarrassed."

Sipowicz sat; so did James, although he did so backward on the chair, leaning his arms along the top of it.

"What have you got to be embarrassed about?" Sipowicz asked flatly. "We never met. You never did nothing to me . . . did you?"

Angelo Giardella's smile was tentative, and wary. "There's something a little sinister about the way you put that, Detective."

James said, "Sunday night, technically early Monday morning, Detective Sipowicz's apartment was busted into."

"I'm sorry to hear that," young Giardella said.

Sipowicz said nothing, just glowered at the young gangster.

"This is of special concern," James said, "because

Detective Sipowicz, and his wife, were both at home at the time. And these men had guns."

"They weren't there to raid the icebox," Sipowicz said.

"Shots were fired," James said. "Nobody was hurt, fortunately."

"Except I did slash the arm of one of 'em," Sipowicz said.

"And then they got away," James said, "these two men with guns."

"I'm not sure I follow this," Angelo Giardella said.

James removed a folded-up circular from his shirt pocket; opening it up, he tossed it in front of Giardella.

"Those are the men," James said.

Sipowicz just kept glowering at young Giardella, who was putting his wireframe glasses back on to have a better look.

"I don't know them," he said, after a fairly long study. "Is it your thinking that these are professional killers?"

James nodded, saying, "That would be our inclination, yes."

Sipowicz, as if spitting out a seed, said, "Why 'embarrassed,' before."

Swallowing, young Giardella again removed the wireframes and said, "Because of what Alfonse Giardella did to you."

"Oh, you mean, shot me?"

". . . Yes. He wasn't a very . . . ethical man. He embarrassed my family, particularly where our business associates are concerned."

"You mean, by ratting them out."

"Yes. I'm aware that the two of you had a rather long-standing feud. . . ."

Sipowicz snorted a laugh. "I busted your uncle rollin' drunks in Tompkins Square Park, my first year on."

Angelo Giardella shifted rather uncomfortably in the booth. "He wasn't my uncle, actually. He was my father's cousin. We were second cousins. I knew him only from family occasions. Now, he was a self-made man, and I admire that . . . rising from the kind of activities you first arrested him for, to erecting a large and successful private business—"

"Erecting, that's the right word."

"—which he, and his wife, who was his secretary and business partner, ran very profitably for many years. Nonetheless, all that said—I consider Alfonse Giardella an embarrassment."

Sipowicz wasn't used to hearing wiseguys use words like "nonetheless." This kid sounded more like a mob lawyer than a mob guy who needed one.

Sipowicz sneered. "Yet you're followin' in his footsteps."

Angelo Giardella's smile was patient, and a little melancholy. "Detective Sipowicz, if I were following in my second cousin's footsteps, we'd have met before now, you and I. You know, you can't pick what family you're born into. Some of us are lucky enough to be born with a silver spoon in our mouths . . . mine just happened to be slightly tarnished."

James said, "There are positive things being said

about you, Mr. Giardella. They say you're running your dirty business clean, these days."

He shrugged, slightly. "I entered the family business. As it happens, my family business is entertainment . . . specifically, adult entertainment."

"By adult," Sipowicz said, "we're talking about the world of whack-off."

He didn't flinch. "Yes. Dance clubs, publishing erotica and so on."

"Peep shows and hardcore videos and jerk-off mags and titty bars, kind of thing, is that the family business you mean?"

The young porn prince did seem vaguely embarrassed, but he didn't avert Sipowicz's gaze. "You know it is. We serve a human need."

"You oughta put in for one of them Nobel piece-of-ass prizes."

"What I have done to deserve this disdain, detective?"

Sipowicz hardly knew what to make of this guy. Disdain? What kind of word was that, for a wiseguy to use?

James said, "Maybe nothing, Mr. Giardella. But considerable time has been spent examining Detective Sipowicz's past cases. You know, looking for someone who might possibly hold the kind of grudge that could be behind this incident."

Angelo Giardella looked from James to Sipowicz, slowly, and back again; then, with careful consideration, said, "Are you recording this conversation?"

Sipowicz snorted. "You see a freakin' tape recorder?"

"That wasn't what I asked."

"No," James said, "we're not recording this conversation."

"Because I would like to be able to speak frankly."

"We would like you to do that," James said.

Sipowicz nodded, said, "This is just between us girls."

With a sigh, Angelo Giardella said. "My business may skirt the law at times. We of course push the envelope where 'blue laws' are concerned, all the time. For example, many newsstand magazines, currently, depict ejaculation."

Sipowicz glanced at James and said, "He means 'come shots,' kid."

"Really?" James said. "Newsstand magazines?"

"With the mainstream publishing material like that," Angelo Giardella said, wearily, "the adult entertainment trade has to . . . try harder."

"Every business has its ups and downs," Sipowicz said.

Now the close-set eyes tightened. "But I assure you we are not venturing into the questionable waters occasionally traversed by my second cousin."

Traversed? They weren't kidding when they said this kid went to college.

"Every model or actress we employ is eighteen years of age—no more providing the Traci Lordses of this world with fake I.D.s. In fact, we're scrupulous about examining what the girls present to us as identification."

Sipowicz grunted a laugh. "I bet you are."

"We do not produce or traffic in kiddie porn or

any other extreme materials. The girls in our clubs are dancers, not prostitutes; if they're caught attempting to solicit, by our people, they're out on their pretty behinds."

Such language.

"What's perhaps more important, the money from Giardella Entertainment Enterprises is not filtered into organized crime–type activities. The money doesn't go into loan-sharking or drug-trafficking or any of what *may* have happened in the past, under the old management."

James said, "You mentioned Mrs. Giardella, before. If she played such a big role in the business, why didn't she take over?"

Angelo Giardella lowered his head, respectfully. "She's very ill. She's had a series of strokes, and is hospitalized. In many regards, she was the one in the family with the business sense."

"Alfonse had the people skills," Sipowicz smirked.

Some defiance found its way into young Giardella's expression, and his tone. "You see, detectives, whether you like it or not, whether what we trade in meets your moral standards, this *is* a family business—not 'family' in the mob sense, but in the sense that there are moms and dads and grandpas and grandmas and cousins and sisters and brothers. We're not monsters. Just immigrants and their offspring, who tried to assimilate. And I like to think I'm putting the finishing, legitimizing touches on that decades-long, generations-spanning endeavor."

"You oughta run for office, kid," Sipowicz said.

"You got the line of bull for it . . . and you grew up around crime. You'd make a perfect politician."

"There's no need to be insulting," he said.

James asked, "Did you ever do business with Frank Dellacroce?"

Young Giardella blinked, caught off-guard by that one. "No. I know of him. He's in prison."

"Was he a business partner of your second cousin's?"

"No. Why do you ask?"

"You don't ask the questions," Sipowicz said. "We ask the questions. You may be the new clean-cut generation who wants his business to be family without a capital letter on the front, but to me, you're still a pus-pimple living off other's people's weakness and misery, you just happen to be a pus-pimple in an Armani suit. The money you're building your new morally improved business on did come outta underage girls, one of which your second cousin murdered when she was gonna come forward with her story, which coulda got him nailed on kiddie porn; it's filthy dirty money that come from loan sharks and prostitution and hijacking, and about the only good thing I can say about you is, I like you better than I did your second cousin, may he fry in fucking hell."

"I didn't send these men after you, detective," Angelo Giardella said, calmly, tapping on the circular. "Much as you may miss my late second cousin, and long for your symbiotic relationship, I am not him. And you have no reason to be in my life."

Sipowicz pointed a finger at him, like a gun. "You want to keep it that way."

"Could I hang on to this?" young Giardella asked James, lifting the circular. "If I find something out, I'll let you know."

"We'd appreciate that," James said, and handed him his card, and got up.

"Symbiotic my ass," Sipowicz said, getting up, looking down at the fashion-model pornographer. "You think I *miss* your fat-ass rug-wearin' second cousin? You're full of shit."

"Maybe so," young Giardella said. "But the funny thing . . . nothing."

"What? What?"

A tiny shrug. "You remind me of him."

And Angelo Giardella returned to his computer printouts, while James Martinez guided a stunned Andy Sipowicz away from the booth and out of Minetta's, before the anger could explode.

NINE

At the end of his second evening of bodyguarding Laura Wynn—which had been very pleasant duty so far, for Bobby Simone—he consented when she asked him to escort her to the penthouse suite where she and her father lived, and her mother had been killed.

The latter subject came up almost immediately upon entering the marble foyer when, arm in arm with her "retinue," Laura (again wearing a black turtleneck and jeans and those clunky boots) asked him to go into the kitchen and get them some sodas, on ice.

"I'll meet you in my father's study," she said, with a nod in that direction, making her blond hair—which she'd worn down, tonight, full and brushing her shoulders—shimmer under the light of the chandelier. "It's as close to cozy as this marble icebox gets."

"Won't your father mind?"

"He's away till tomorrow afternoon. Some sort of board meeting in Philadelphia, and it's the butler's night off, too." Her full lips pursed into a wicked kiss of a smile. "We're two naughty children . . . with the grown-ups away."

"Okay. What kind of soda? Which way's the kitchen?"

She frowned, cutely. "You ask so many questions. What are you, a cop?"

"Why don't you just come along . . . help me get some glasses and ice. . . ."

She let go of his arm, shook her head, which did wonderful things to all that blond hair. But her expression was grave, and a little spooked.

"I don't go in there. That's where . . . where the burglar killed my mother."

It was the most directly she'd spoken of it.

"Sorry," he said. "Just point the way, then."

She did.

When he entered the blindingly white kitchen—which was about as large as his entire TriBeCa apartment—it seemed oddly familiar, its cupboards with etched-glass faces, the elaborate island with multi-burner stove and sink and counterspace. Then he realized that this eerie familiarity came from his having seen photographs and videotape of it as a crime scene, and not because he was a New York City police detective, either: everyone in the city (and much of the country) had seen this crime scene on the tube, that spacious white kitchen, its white tile floor splashed with blood, decorated with a dead body outline.

In the blond-paneled, white-shuttered study, she was stretched on the green velvet cushions of the couch, in her stocking feet (black socks, too); but she got into a sitting position, making room for him, as she took the glass of Diet Coke on ice he offered her.

The sofa was comfy but firm. He sipped his own Coke and said, "Is that what you think happened, Laura?"

She smiled, eyes crinkling in confusion. "What?"

"That a burglar killed your mother. I know the defense tried to float that theory."

Her mouth flinched in irritation. "Is that why you think I invited you here? To talk about my mother's death? Do you share the same morbid curiosity as the rest of the city?"

He gave her a mild, restrained smile. "Now *you're* the one asking a lot of questions. Hey, cut me a break—I'm a cop, and I'm at the scene of the most famous, controversial crime in recent history. I think I did pretty good not bringing it up till now."

Her expression softened. "I suppose so. I'll tell you what I think, but then let's close the book on it, okay?"

"Okay."

She fixed the light blue eyes on him; it was like looking down into very clear water, but water so deep you weren't sure what you were seeing. "My father would never kill my mother. She might have killed *him*, in a fit of rage . . . I saw her hit him, often enough, in drunken fury . . . but he never raised a hand to her."

Simone shrugged a shoulder. "But sometimes people snap. Sometimes enough is enough."

"Self-defense, you mean," she said, nodding, but not in agreement, rather in the manner of someone who has heard something all too many times.

"Mother raised a knife, and he took it away, got those cuts on his hands, and killed her."

"Sure. He could have walked if he said that."

Her face tightened. "But that wasn't the truth. And Daddy did walk, anyway, didn't he? I know the vast unwashed public would love to have it otherwise, but my father did not kill my mother. It may be terribly dull to think a burglar did it, it would make a far less dramatic TV mini-series, but that is what I am convinced happened."

"Nothing was stolen—"

"Mother obviously interrupted the thief before he'd taken anything . . . and once the murder occurred, he panicked and left."

This time he shrugged with his eyebrows. "Possible."

"How open-minded," she smirked. "And now we've exhausted a topic that seems designed to drain all the fun out of this evening."

His grin was shy and had some shame in it. "Sorry. I didn't mean to be insensitive about your tragedy."

Her smirk softened in a nice smile. "Apology accepted."

"And it was a fun evening. I almost feel guilty getting paid . . . almost."

She moved closer to him, and a giddiness came into her voice as she said, "It was *good* tonight, wasn't it?"

They'd done a straight run-through of *The Star-Wagon* (which was the name of the play), with the notes waiting for the end—and there hadn't been many notes from the obviously pleased director.

"I like it a lot," he said. "You guys are playing it great."

"I'm glad you think so. You know, with dated material, it's so easy to overplay. Just giving it a nice, low-key, realistic read makes it go down smoother, don't you think?"

"Definitely. Was that your aunt I saw there? I thought I recognized her, from TV."

Midway through the rehearsal, Constance Reed, in a black turtleneck and black ski pants, an outfit echoing her niece's wardrobe, sneaked in the back of the theater and took a side seat, watching. Between scenes, Laura came down and sat with her aunt, and they exchanged intense, whispered words; they had not, however, exchanged kisses and/or hugs—there had been a real air of turmoil about it. And then the aunt had left.

"Yes, that was my aunt," Laura said. "Connie always takes an interest in my work."

Simone had, of course, recognized Constance Reed, and not just from "Hollywood Squares." He was well aware that Diane Russell and Greg Medavoy had spoken with Laura's aunt—and that the conversation had turned hostile.

Keeping his tone casual, he asked, "Was she giving you some pointers?"

"Tell you the truth, she was a little upset because some police came around and bothered her today."

"What about?"

She turned the light blue eyes on him, a cool, even

chilly gaze. "About that subject we're not discussing any further."

He sipped his Coke, frowning a little, playing dumb. "I wonder why they'd be talking to her about that, at this late date."

She frowned, too, and there was irritation and sarcasm in her tone. "Why don't you ask them? They're your friends, aren't they?"

Did she know Diane and Greg were from his precinct?

"Hey," he said, a shrug, a smile, "it's a big department, Laura. We're not all pals, and I'm not exactly kept informed of every investigation."

She looked down into the glass of Coke, then lifted her head and her expression was chagrined. "I don't mean to be bitchy. Does it seem to you I'm always being bitchy?"

"Not in the least. Does it seem like I'm always asking nosy questions?"

"No. Maybe a little, tonight."

A half smile twitched in his cheek. "I've just never been around, you know, actors before. Somebody you saw on TV is suddenly right there in front of you. Kinda weird."

She seemed a little flattered, now. "Had you seen me on TV? 'Law and Order,' maybe?"

Everybody had seen her on TV—and her father, and her late mother, with the coverage of the murder case.

But he said, "I don't watch much TV. But I saw you in that Mel Gibson movie."

She was a good actress, but her false modesty was apparent as she said, "Tiny part."

He'd seen the movie, but didn't remember her in it.

"You made an impression," he said, hoping she wouldn't ask him anything specific about it. "I saw your aunt in lots of things."

"Some people think she's kind of a joke, but she's really quite an accomplished performer."

He slipped an arm around her. "Were you two close?"

"Very. I mean, it's obvious, isn't it? She's where I could go for the support my mother wouldn't give me, and my father couldn't give me."

"You mean, like tips about acting and so on?"

"Sure," she said, but she was shaking her head, no, as she said it, "only, more like emotional support. She's a very warm person, my aunt."

Yet tonight aunt and niece hadn't touched; if anything, there seemed to be a wall between them, as if the only thing that brought them together was some common crisis.

"It's good to have somebody to talk to," he said.

She snuggled closer, nestling in his shoulder. "Yes it is."

He kissed her forehead. "Must've been important, having your aunt there for you, when you lost your mom."

"Yes."

"I know it can be pretty tough."

"You say that like . . . like you know, Bobby."

He nodded.

She drew away, just a little, to look at him, more carefully. "You lost somebody, didn't you?"

He nodded again.

"Who, Bobby?"

". . . My wife."

"She's . . . dead?"

Another nod.

"How long?"

"Coming up on two years. Sounds like a long time, when I say it."

Her eyes tightened with sympathy. "But it doesn't feel like a long time. . . ."

"No."

"What was her name?"

"Maria."

"Pretty name."

He smiled. "Like the song."

"How did she die?"

"Breast cancer. She came home from work one day, said she was sick, and she just never got better."

"Oh, Bobby . . ."

"That's why I didn't come up the other night. I'm still not one hundred percent, in the emotions area, myself."

"I understand." She began to smile. "You want to have a laugh? Real hoot?"

"Sure."

"Come with me," she said, standing, taking and tugging his hand like one child leading another. She dragged him out of the study and across the formal living room and around and up the winding staircase. She then deposited him in the hallway, outside the door, which she opened and did a little mock bow and a "Price Is Right" hand gesture. He peeked in.

It was a child's bedroom, a dainty, frilly, Victorian world of pink and white.

"Go on in," she said, "if you want a laugh."

He stepped inside and she followed, closing the door. The carpet was as fluffy as egg whites, the walls cotton-candy pink. A white fourposter bed had a pink canopy and pink-and-blue floral bedspread, and the furnishings—dresser, bedstand, and a student desk with a hutch whose shelves had on display marionettes and little porcelain figures, all wearing harlequin faces—were white with brass handles. The drapes were white and pure and ruffly as a child's confirmation dress, and in one corner at a small table sat stuffed animals, a teddy bear, a boy clown, a girl clown, and a tiger, frozen in a perpetual afternoon tea party.

The room was not small—no rooms in this penthouse were, the closets could have passed for apartments in some parts of the city—but the featured attraction of the room made it seem small. To the left, taking up a large corner of the room, was an ornate Victorian dollhouse, four feet high, obviously handcrafted and beautifully so. The back of the house was facing front, with its fabulous interior exposed—delicately scaled-down furnishings, brocade wallpaper, father, mother, and daughter dolls dressed in the finery of the era, seated at a mahogany diningroom table while an immaculately uniformed black maid doll served them. A perfect family in a perfect world.

"This was your room," Simone said.

"Oh, it still is," she said.

"You're kidding."

"Yes and no." She moved across the fluffy carpet and sat on the edge of the bed; she was in her bare feet, now. "This is my bedroom, but I've been sleeping in a guest bedroom."

He swiveled his head around, eyeing the pink-and-white wonderland. "I didn't figure anybody *really* lived in here."

"My father expected me to. Can you imagine?" She shook her head, patted the spot on the bedspread next to her for him to sit down. He did, and the top of his head brushed the pink cloth of the canopy.

"Picture me coming out of rehab," she continued, "and my father wants me to move into my old bedroom. And, I guess, be his perfect little girl again."

"Why is this room like this?"

"You mean, like it's ready for the next museum tour group to come through?" She shrugged. "Sort of a shrine. To my perfect childhood."

"*Was* it perfect?"

A half smile dimpled her face. "Well, it wasn't bad. Don't let anybody tell you being a rich kid is a rough ride. Look around you—they spoiled me silly. And I was as adorable as Shirley Temple, and just as precocious, and boy, were my parents proud of me."

"Including your mom?"

"Sure! My theatrical ways were cute—in a kid. I was talented! And parents love that: recitals, plays, concerts, pageants. It wasn't till I grew up and wanted to continue in that vein that I became a problem child."

"So then, you and your mom, you *were* close, when you were young?"

She shook her head. "Not really. Let me put it this way—the dollhouse was her idea. She had a collection of Barbies when she was a kid . . . she still does . . . or did. It's displayed in our place in the Hamptons."

"So the dollhouse, that was her toy."

"Yeah. But, then, so was I."

"What do you mean?"

"I mean I was just another doll. A trophy."

"Till you started having a mind of your own."

She nodded. "That was in junior high, and I got sent off to private school, and never lived at home again, except summers, and mostly we weren't here in the summers . . . so this room got frozen. My mom froze it. It was a monument to the past, to the well-behaved child she lost."

"Maybe it's a kind of compliment."

"Maybe. But can you believe how out of touch my father is? Didn't he know the head trip he was sending me on, putting me back in this pink padded cell? That's the kind of thing that makes you *start* drinking."

"Maybe he wanted to put you two on the starwagon."

That made her smile. "A time machine back to when I was more manageable? Before bad things happened?"

Who wouldn't want to take that ride?

"I guess," he said, "it's pretty common for a father to think of his daughter as a little girl."

"I suppose." She had an expression as frozen as the room, but then it melted into something mischievous. "Of course, something that *does* occur to me . . ."

"What's that?"

Those clear blue eyes might have belonged to a doll. "Maybe if it means so much to him, I ought to use this room. As a bedroom, I mean."

"Yeah?"

"Yeah . . ."

And she kissed him. Deeply. Her tongue probing, gently, then thrusting, and he caught her up in his arms, and they fell onto the soft, soft bed, his hands sliding up onto her breasts.

"Gimme a second," she murmured.

Then she slipped off the bed and clicked on the small lamp by the bed, padding over to hit the wall switch, sending the room into a pink-tinged subdued lighting scheme that complimented her skin tone as she pulled the black turtleneck up and over her head, revealing a cotton camisole, and her breasts were so full, they didn't flatten out when she slipped the flimsy underthing over her head. She unzipped the jeans, stepped out of them, and when she kicked them away, he caught sight of the perfectly dimpled twin globes of her behind, too generous a behind for current tastes perhaps, and probably the bane of her existence as an actress, but what a lovely full behind it was.

She still had the panties on as she climbed onto the bed, and as he began unbuttoning his shirt, she tugged at his zipper, and her hand slipped inside, and he was kissing her when his nostrils filled with that familiar perfume, and suddenly he pulled away.

"No . . . not yet," he said.

She frowned, confused. "Not yet?"

"Too soon."

"You mean . . . because of your wife . . ." She stroked his face with one hand, elsewhere with the other. "I'll make you forget, honey, I'll make you forget—"

He sat up. "No. It's not right. I'm working for your father."

"Fuck him! And fuck me."

But it felt wrong, beautiful as she was, and later that night, in his bed, alone, in his apartment, he would lie awake, hard with the thought of her, wondering how he could do that, how he could walk away from that beautiful willing woman, wondering what she would do if he drove back there and knocked on that penthouse door. . . .

Right now, however, he was pushing her hand away, trying to be gentle, zipping his pants, saying, "I'm sorry . . . it's just too soon."

"You bastard!" Her eyes were filled with hurt and fury. "To hell with you! Get out of here! Get out of my house!"

She got off the bed and pulled her pants on, and she was shivering with rage, muttering obscenities at him as he moved past her and got the hell out of there, as she requested.

Too soon. Too soon.

But his wife had nothing to do with it.

It was Diane.

TEN

Diane Russell normally did not dine out in restaurants as trendy, and expensive, as La Paella in SoHo's historic Cast-Iron District. Nor did her "date," Greg Medavoy, who was studying the menu as if it were a clue he couldn't grasp in a criminal investigation he didn't fathom.

"I thought this was supposed to be a Spanish restaurant," he said.

They were seated in the outdoor, sidewalk café-style section of the hole-in-the-wall bistro, at one of only three linen-covered tables, each with its own red-as-a-bullfighter's-cape canopy. One of the tables, situated between the other two, was marked with a RESERVED sign; the third table had another couple not accustomed to prices like La Paella's: James Martinez and Adrianne Lesniak.

"It's not that kind of Spanish restaurant," Russell said.

She had dressed up, a little, for the evening; the casual, undercoverish attire she wore to work might make her stick out here. Her gray ribbed turtleneck and matching trousers would be more appropriate, and yet still give her plenty of freedom of movement, if need be. The burgundy jacket slung over the chair behind her would stay there, for now. Greg's gray suit seemed a little snappier than usual, too; his black and gray tie even had a deco-ish design that he wouldn't normally wear on the job.

They were in the heart of a former warehouse district turned center of upscale shops, art galleries, and pricey restaurants. It was approaching eight in the evening, dusk painting the world a cool blue, with a lovely whisper of a breeze, sidewalks bustling, couples mostly, straight and gay, Yuppie and artsy and occasionally touristy; with the moderately traveled cobblestone streets, in the shadow of six- and seven-story buildings with their beautifully restored cast-iron facades, this was a perfect setting for a romantic evening out.

"What k-kind of Spanish restaurant doesn't have tacos and enchiladas?" Greg wondered.

"That's a Mexican restaurant."

"There's a difference?"

"Quite a few. Start with the prices."

He lifted an eyebrow. "You got a point. What do you suppose zar-zoo-ella dee mary-scoughs is?"

"I think that's a seafood casserole with lobster. We shouldn't order anything, really, except coffee."

Which they already had.

Greg's close-set eyes tightened as he leaned across the table. "I think it would be, you know, more r-r-realistic if we were at least munching on a taco or something. What do you suppose a tapa is? You think that's a misprint? Could be a taco."

"I don't think so."

She glanced at James, stiff in a white shirt and blue tie and the dark blue suit that he probably wore to mass, and Adrianne, slumped in a light blue denim pantsuit with sparkly appliqués, an outfit that Donna Abandando had loaned her. James and Adrianne both had rather glazed smiles and were avoiding each other's eyes; it seemed to make them awkward, being away from a work situation, and in a social one, even a fake social one like this.

This was hardly a date. It was, in fact, a stakeout, and a very controlled one—a mousetrap, actually, using La Paella's acclaimed cuisine for cheese.

The have-you-seen-this-man flier with the mug shot of Leonard Parsons and his hawk-faced associate had been circulated to any hotel and/or restaurant in Manhattan that might be considered by anyone's definition "upscale." Russell and Medavoy had been following up on the resulting calls, several of which proved false alarms; twice, restaurant personnel I.D.ed the suspect (Parsons seemed to dine alone, his partner in crime never accompanying him) but no second sightings at either restaurant had been reported, as yet. As a connoisseur of the finer things, Parsons apparently never dined at the same place twice.

La Paella was not necessarily an exception; but a man who may have been Parsons had stopped during the lunch hour, declined the forty-five-minute wait, and instead made a reservation for tonight. The manager—who also served as maître d', and who happened to be Middle Eastern—had seen the resemblance to the photo on the circular, and called the 15th Precinct.

Diane and Greg had set up the trap for tonight, utilizing the outdoor cafélike area, because it was a controlled environment, away from the other restaurant patrons. On the other hand, pedestrians were walking by, and the guy would have a straight shot at the street, if he made a break. So it wasn't ideal.

"They got paella," Greg said. "I know what that is. It's this rice dish."

"Mmm-hmm."

Across the street, in an unmarked van, two more detectives waited in case things got out of hand, Gotelli and Morrisey from the 4 to 12 shift.

"I could order that," Greg said, considering it, nodding at the very possibility of something familiar on this menu. "You would think that would be a specialty, probably, since it's the name of the place."

"You'd think."

"I wonder if they make it with sugar. I'm avoiding sugar."

"Why would they make it with sugar?"

"Y-you'd be surprised what they put sugar in, in these places. And with my allergies, with you know, these f-f-foreign spices and herbs, I take my life in my hands, eating out."

"Here's our man."

Greg may have been a seriously confused human being—craving tacos and enchiladas even as he worried about sugar intake and allergies—but he was nonetheless a damn good cop. He didn't look up from the menu as the slender dark manager, in white shirt, string tie and black pants, looking just a little nervous, led Leonard Parsons to his table, retreating a bit too quickly back into his restaurant.

Stocky, with a round pasty face, small, dark, dead eyes and a mustache, Parsons, looking vaguely priestlike in a black suit with a black T-shirt, settled into his chair, studying the menu with the intensity of a scientist going over key data.

"Jeez, he looks a little like Andy," Greg whispered.

"Andy says the guy's his evil twin."

Greg smiled at her, as if he were making pleasant conversation. "Now looks like as good a time as any."

Smiling back the same way, Russell, whose back was to the guy, nodded. "Cue James."

Greg did, nodding.

And James nudged his coffee cup off the table, sending it to the cement, shattering.

Parsons turned toward the exploding cup, and Greg was on one side of him, Russell the other, each grabbing an arm, Greg handling the cuffs, snapping them on, and Parsons started to rise, bumping into the table, making the silverware rattle, his tiny eyes wide in the white moon-face as he got to his feet, hands cuffed suddenly behind him.

But there was no indignation, and only the merest surprise. He just looked from Greg to Diane and back again, with blank, almost bland indifference.

"You're under arrest, Mr. Parsons," Russell said.

Greg read him his rights, and James and Adrianne moved in until the hit man was circled by cops. It had gone down quietly, with little fuss, but there'd been enough noise to attract some attention, the cup shattering, the table getting jarred, not to mention Parsons standing there in handcuffs. So Adrianne had to hold up her shield and instruct the gawkers to move along, police business.

"You could've at least waited till I ordered," Parsons said hoarsely, with a faint sneer worthy of Sipowicz's evil twin.

Russell said, "We'll microwave you a burrito at the stationhouse."

Greg's eyes lighted up. "There's an idea."

And with James doing the hauling, they led him to the waiting van across the street.

The sign over the door read A REST ROOM, but this wasn't a john, though it was a room where many a dirty soul had come clean; a long time ago, an R had fallen out of the word ARREST, and no one had ever bothered replacing it. Interview Two was how the detectives of the One Five referred to the Arrest Room, a square chamber that seemed narrow because the facing wall, as you came in, was largely taken up by a steel holding cell, with seating for five.

At right, the wall by the fingerprinting station bore a spreading smudgy blossom of black where excess ink from the rollers was rolled off. At the far left, the wall was mostly a mirror—two-way glass, designed for protecting witnesses during line-ups; at the moment, Sylvia Costas was behind that mirror, watching.

Against the wall that faced the holding cell was a metal desk with a typewriter, for taking statements, and a metal bookcase lined with various forms, which came in handy in this blue-green confessional. Taking up most of the space, centrally, was a long narrow table, at which Leonard Parsons—a man in black, hands folded prayerfully before him—sat silently. He was at the head of the table, but he wasn't in charge.

Russell sat next to Parsons, with her back to the holding cell. Greg was seated across from her.

Russell said to the prisoner, "This could go well for you."

Greg said to him, "Better than it should."

"Can I smoke in here?" Parsons asked. From the ragged, hoarse sound of his voice, a cigarette was the last thing he needed.

"Sure."

"They took my cigarettes away from me when they took my billfold and everything."

"We'll get you some," Russell said. "Greg?"

Greg nodded and left.

"I need to make a phone call," Parsons said.

"You want a lawyer, that's your right."

He smirked. "No kidding."

"But maybe you want to explore other options first."

He faced forward, staring straight ahead, his expression blank. "I need to make a phone call."

"You want a cigarette or a phone call?"

"I want both. I didn't know it was an either or."

"It isn't. But let me give you a word of friendly advice . . . you want to listen to your options, here, first."

"I need to make a phone call."

Russell shrugged, smiled, raised her eyebrows. "This precinct, this is where Detective Sipowicz works out of. We're family, here."

"I need to make a phone call."

She leaned forward. "You do remember Detective Sipowicz? The man you tried to kill?"

"I need to make a phone call."

"Or was it Sylvia Costas you were trying to kill?"

"I need to make a phone call."

Russell leaned back in her chair, didn't look at him as she spoke, almost absently. "You only have one prior conviction. You can go away for a long time, on attempted murder. Of course, with a little cooperation, that attempted murder rap might go away. Maybe we'd just be talking home invasion and ADW charges."

"I need to make a phone call."

"Who knows? Get really cooperative and maybe the ADW charge goes away."

"I need . . . how?"

He had turned toward her on that last word. His round white face remained expressionless, but the dead eyes were suddenly alive.

"Names," Russell said. "Your intended victim, your accomplice, your employer. Tell us who hired you, and why."

"I think I should discuss this with an attorney."

"An assistant district attorney is on the way over here right now."

"That's not what I mean by an attorney. I need to make a phone call."

Greg came in, shut the door behind him, held out an open pack of Camels to the prisoner.

"Thanks," Parsons said.

Greg lighted him up off a book of matches.

Parsons blew smoke out. "I need to make a phone call."

Russell said to Greg, "He wants to make a phone call."

Greg said, "That's his prerogative."

"I had a cell phone," Parsons said, "but they took it away from me. With my cigarettes. And my billfold."

"Around here we don't put phones in the cells," Greg said, and smiled, proud of himself for the remark.

"I'm not some lowlife mope off the streets," Parsons said, looking at Greg. "I'm an educated man. I know my rights. I would like my phone call."

The door opened and Sylvia Costas slipped into the room. Small briefcase in hand, she wore a brown suit with a brown silk blouse, very business-like for someone who had been bothered at home and asked to come in at short notice. But this, of course, was a special case for Sylvia Costas.

"This is our riding A.D.A.," Russell said, gesturing to Sylvia.

Greg rose, gave Sylvia his chair, and took the next chair down, like a guest on a talk show.

"I need to make a phone call," Parsons said.

Sylvia was her usual perfectly composed self; every hair in place, eyes as cool and blue as a mountain stream. Leonard Parsons might have been just another in a long line of routine defendants.

And if Leonard Parsons recognized Sylvia as his intended victim, he didn't show it. If she'd been his target, he was one cool, cold customer.

"If you don't want to talk to me without a lawyer present," Sylvia said, "legal representation can be arranged."

"I need to make a phone call."

"Fine." She rose. "Inform your attorney the charges will include attempted murder and conspiracy to commit murder."

Sylvia was to the door when Parsons said, "What considerations might I get, if I cooperate now?"

Sylvia's facial shrug was as eloquent as it was slight. "Immunity isn't out of the question."

"For telling who hired me."

Sylvia came over and sat down, placing her briefcase on the table before her. "We can start with who your target was."

He twitched half a smile. "Well, it wasn't the wife."

"Detective Sipowicz was your target."

"That's right."

"You were there to kill him."

Worry came into Parsons's eyes. "I'm not saying that. I haven't said that. . . . This is a mistake."

"You're doing fine, Mr. Parsons—"

"I already talked too much. Look, I'm not comfortable without that phone call."

"We're not trying to infringe on your rights, Mr.

Parsons." She rose again. "Let him have his phone call."

"Certainly, Mrs. Sipowicz," Greg said.

Parsons frowned. "What was that?"

"Thank you, Detective," Sylvia said to Greg. "but I prefer Ms. Costas. I'm staying with that professionally."

Parsons, panic apparent, said to Sylvia, "*What's* your name?"

"I'm sorry, Ms. Costas," Greg said, with an embarrassed little smile. "I won't make that mistake in the future."

His cage well and truly rattled, Parsons said, "Who the hell are you, lady?"

Sylvia was at the door, now, just about to go out. With a smile that might have accompanied an invitation to tea, and in a tone of voice as gentle and musical as a windchime, she said, "Sylvia Costas Sipowicz."

The tiny dark eyes tightened, and Parsons looked from her to the two cops and back. "What the hell are you people trying to pull?"

Innocently, still poised at the door, Sylvia asked, "Is my name familiar to you?"

He sneered at her. "You know it is."

"Maybe you'd feel more comfortable with another representative of the district attorney's office."

He grunted a humorless laugh. "You think?"

"I can understand you thinking that you might get better terms from a more . . . dispassionate party."

He stared ahead, again. "I want my phone call."

Sylvia turned to Russell. "Call Leo Cohen in. And,

of course, you'll want to keep Mr. Parsons protected until his representation arrives."

"Sure thing," Russell said. "Greg, check and see if Detective Sipowicz is handy, would you? He can guard our prisoner."

Parson's pale face turned paler.

"That would be an efficient use of our time," Greg said, "seeing as how Detective Sipowicz is also a witness and could make an identification of the suspect. If, for example, we've made a terrible mistake, and this isn't the man who broke into the Sipowicz apartment at all, who better than Detective Sipowicz to rectify that miscarriage of justice?"

Russell didn't bother suppressing her smile; she was proud of Greg—a beautiful array of words and not a stammer in the bunch.

And of course, Andy wasn't in the house (Sylvia said he'd gone out on some personal matter), but the prisoner didn't know that.

"I want the details of the deal," Parsons said.

"Okay," Sylvia said, and within half an hour, a deal had been worked out. Or seemingly had, until a major stumbling block presented itself.

"I won't give up my partner," Parsons said, moving his head from side to side. "I want that understood."

Sylvia sighed, gestured with an open hand. "Immunity is only possible with complete cooperation."

He didn't look at her as he spoke. "I don't even know his name."

"You don't know your partner's name."

"I don't have his address, either. I don't know where he's staying."

"You don't know where your partner is staying?"

Now Parsons looked right at her; there was something frantic in the eyes of this formerly cool killer. "He's not my partner. I never worked with him before."

"Then why don't you want to give him up?"

He turned away again. "Business ethics. Professional courtesy."

Russell, who was way ahead of Sylvia on this one, said, "Could I have a word with you in the hall, Ms. Costas?"

Sylvia looked at Russell for a moment; there seemed, in the A.D.A.'s eyes, to be a flicker of irritation at having her interrogation interrupted in this fashion. Russell had sensed a tension between herself and Sylvia of late, and wondered if it had something to do with the time Andy had been spending with her, helping Diane deal with her alcohol problem. She had asked Andy about it but he'd only said, "No, Sylvia's fine with that."

But then Sylvia nodded, and soon the two women were outside the door, having an impromptu confab.

"If I'm not overstepping my bounds and getting into your business," Russell said, "I'd suggest you give him a pass, on that one."

Sylvia seemed not to believe what she was hearing. "Surely you'd like to bring in his accomplice—"

"Yes, and we will. But we found a picture in Parsons' billfold. Come take a look."

At her desk, Russell showed Sylvia the plastic-bagged photo: it was Parsons with his arm around a hawk-faced man, clearly the second intruder, the police sketch come to life; they were in swimsuits and the blueness of the shallow water they stood in had to be an ocean. The affection between the two was obvious.

"Oh my God," Sylvia said. "They're lovers."

"Partners in bed *and* business."

Sylvia was smiling, shaking her head. "He's not going to give up his lover. Not easily."

"No."

Now Sylvia looked directly at Russell. "So we should get what we can get."

Russell shrugged. "That's your call. I just bring 'em in. You prosecute them."

Sylvia rolled her eyes. "I can't prosecute this one. We're already on shaky ground, not to mention out in left field. If ever there was a conflict of interest . . ."

"Leo Cohen's on his way here," Russell said. "We'll make it his case."

"Good. I agreed with you and Greg about this as a strategy, to get a good statement out of him; but let's not kid ourselves."

Back in Interview Two, Sylvia said to Parsons, "Let's approach this from another angle."

But Parsons, sitting with his arms folded, staring straight ahead again, had been reflecting.

He said, "I'm thinking maybe I want that phone call, after all. I'm thinking if you put your husband in here with me and he beats the hell out of me, then you're all going to be up on charges and lose your jobs and I'm going to be out on the street, I'm thinking."

Sylvia's voice was calm, almost soothing. "Your partner would be a candidate for immunity, as well."

He looked at her. "Yeah?"

"If we're building a conspiracy case, having two of the co-conspirators testifying against their ringleader is a real benefit."

He frowned in thought. "Two against one kind of thing."

She nodded.

"I'll think about it."

"All right. So . . . who hired you, Mr. Parsons?"

And, with no further hedging or hesitation, Parsons told them.

Sylvia Costas blinked once and then stared at their prisoner with frozen eyes. A similarly stunned Russell looked at Greg, whose expression was not unlike the one he'd worn trying to figure out the La Paella menu.

ELEVEN

Earlier that same evening—about the time Diane Russell and three other detectives were positioning themselves at tables at La Paella—Bobby Simone had met with J. Michael Wynn in his study in the Central Park West penthouse.

"Is there anything I can say or do to make you reconsider?" Wynn asked. The tanned, silver-haired multimillionaire—crisply casual in a light tan polo shirt and white slacks—seated himself behind the blond desk, reached for his checkbook, flipped it open invitingly and said, "Perhaps a bonus that your Mr. Timmons needn't know about?"

"It's not about money." Simone, in a dark blue suit with light blue shirt and dark blue tie that vaguely echoed a police officer's uniform, stood before the desk, like a student in the principal's office. "I think if you talk to your daughter, you'll find she agrees with me."

Wynn winced, smiled. "Agrees in what sense?"

Simone shrugged slightly. "That I'm not right for this job. It got kind of ugly last night, Mr. Wynn."

The smile turned into a concerned frown. "Was she drinking?"

"No."

Relief flooded his features. "Well, she's an only child and spoiled. She can get belligerent if she doesn't get her way, even when she *isn't* drinking."

"She's a very talented young woman, Mr. Wynn. I like her. But I think after last night—"

"What?"

Simone shook his head, no. "I don't see any point in going into that."

"Did you rebuff her? Romantically?"

Simone said nothing. Wynn was staring at him with those same spooky light blue eyes his daughter had; having Laura's eyes stare at him out of her father's face was damn disconcerting.

Wynn said, "You struck her in her Achilles' heel— her ego. All actors have huge egos, inflated egos, but like most balloons full of gas, they're easily punctured."

"You've been decent to me, Mr. Wynn. I'm gonna be straight with you. There's another reason I want to walk away from this job."

Wynn came out around from behind the desk. "Yes?"

"I do like your daughter. But I don't like my motives, here."

Wynn, arms folded, stood facing Simone. "You mean, the fact that you took this job to look for . . . evidence against me?"

Surprised by Wynn's frankness, Simone nodded. "To poke around in your wife's murder case, a little, yes. I'm bothered by that, now."

Wynn's smile was ironic. "Bothered by taking

money from the man you're hoping to get the goods on."

"Yes."

The irony left as Wynn shook his head, his expression reasonable, now. "But I went into this with my eyes wide open, Detective Simone. I knew who you were, and what your ulterior motives would likely be."

Simone frowned. "Then why hire me?"

"For the reasons I previously stated. Your record is beyond reproach, and we're both men who suffered a great loss."

"Don't do that."

"What?"

"Don't use my wife's death to try to manipulate me. It's private and personal and don't do that again."

Wynn raised his hands in surrender. "If that came across as cynical, I apologize."

"If you hoped, by convincing me of your innocence, that I'd somehow pass that along to my partner—"

Wynn's eyes tightened in apparent confusion. "Your partner? That . . . Sipowicz character?"

"Yes."

"The prosecutor's husband."

"Yes. If you thought, by winning me over, I could get the heat taken off of you, you're sadly mistaken."

The light blue eyes appraised him, openly. "Have I?"

"What?"

"Won you over. Do you still believe I killed my wife?"

"No, you haven't won me over. Yeah, I think you probably did."

Wynn's face fell.

Simone continued, "I think it was likely self-defense, though. Not that my opinion matters."

Wynn raised an eyebrow, set it back down. "Well. I respect you for your honesty."

A knock at the study door startled Wynn—the first indication that his calm surface concealed frayed nerves—and he called out, "Yes?"

The door opened a ways and it was the gray-templed black butler, George, who seemed a trifle unnerved himself.

"Sir, there's a police detective here and he insists on seeing you—"

George was still in mid-sentence when Andy Sipowicz, a bear in a rumpled brown suit and green striped tie and blue striped shirt, barged in, barreling past the butler, saying, "Don't blame the help, he told me to wait in the vestibule."

And then Andy saw Simone, and their eyes locked, their expressions froze into mirrored blank disbelief.

Andy's eyes were round in their dark-circled sockets. "What are you doin' here, Bobby?"

Simone was still looking for the words when Wynn said, "He's been working for *me*, Detective Sipowicz."

"Workin' for you?" Andy smiled, finding that ridiculous. "Yeah, right."

But when Simone didn't say anything, Andy's eyes

became slits and he began to strut around a little, gesturing with a finger at Wynn, casually saying to his partner, "You're not really workin' for this asshole?"

Simone put a hand, gently, on his partner's arm. "Andy, let's both get out of here, and I'll explain."

Wynn said, "He's been doing some bodyguard work for me, Detective Sipowicz."

Andy's smile curdled, and he drew his arm away from Simone's grasp. "Hey—tell me this is a joke. Tell me *this* isn't the security job you're doin' for Harry Timmons?"

"It's not like that, Andy—"

"Tell me you ain't puttin' the dick into private dick." Andy's face twitched and he began strutting again, raising his voice. "Tell me I ain't been coverin' for you on the job, so you can pick up a paycheck from the guy who tried to have my wife whacked—"

Wynn said, "I did nothing of the kind. Detective Simone has been providing security for my daughter, if it's any of your business."

"I don't know if it's my business." Hands in his pockets, he planted himself in front of Simone, cocking his head. "What do you think, Bobby? Think it's my business when my partner, my friend, goes to work for some well-heeled uptown son of a bitch who killed his wife?"

Simone closed his eyes and opened them. "Andy . . . not here . . ."

Andy moved away, strutting again. "Y'think my *friend*—my *colleague*—ought to be working for the bastard that hired a couple button guys to redecorate my apartment with nine fucking millimeters?"

Simone was holding up his hands, palms out, trying to calm his partner. "Please, partner—"

Andy whirled and pointed a gunlike finger at Simone. "Don't call me that. Don't you call me that. You just lost the right to call me that."

Wynn said, "If it matters, Detective Simone just tendered his resignation."

Andy threw his hands in the air. "Oh, yeah, that makes it just peachy. Forget what I said before, Bobby. You're a prince among men."

Simone felt sick to his stomach, and sick at heart.

Wynn stepped up to Andy and looked him right in the eye. "I didn't do either of those things you accused me of, Detective Sipowicz. And I'm beginning to gather that you're not here on official business."

Andy, the whiteness of his face accentuated by the tanned face he was nose to nose with, said matter of factly, "The badge got me past the doorman and the security, but yeah, I'm here on my own . . . to give you a free security consultation. And unlike Detective Simone, you won't have to pay me nothin'."

Simone shook his head. "Andy . . ."

Wynn folded his arms, raised his chin. "Speak your piece and leave."

Andy's smile was a one-sided, awful thing. "I'll do that. Tell you what . . . you call off those two clowns you hired. Call 'em off, now. And maybe I won't kill your ass."

Wynn's face went almost as pale as Andy's. "I didn't hire anyone—"

Andy held a thick finger up. "Anybody looks cross-eyed at my wife, she gets a suspicious hangnail, she even has a bad dream, you answer for it."

Wynn swallowed and backed away. "I suggest you leave, detective."

Andy grabbed Wynn by the front of his polo shirt, both fists filled with tan cloth. "Call off your dogs. Understand? Send Leonard Parsons and his pal back to the Windy City."

Wynn's eyes were wide with terror, now. "I don't know what you're *talking* about!"

"Lawyers and connections and money, they won't save you this time . . ."

Simone put a hand on Andy's shoulder.

Andy glanced at it with disgust; but he reserved the bulk of his contempt for Wynn. "I'll pick the time and place, scumbag. Like some poor homeless bastard dead in the gutter, you'll be just another DOA."

Brushing Simone's hand off his shoulder, as if it were an annoying insect, Andy—shaking his lowered head—stalked out.

"You heard him threaten me," Wynn said, trembling, breathing hard. "You're a witness!"

"No I'm not," Simone said, wondering if he should try to catch up with Andy, explain himself. But the sick feeling, the awful knowledge that Andy had so easily thought the worst of him, kept Simone from doing it.

"I'll accept your resignation," Wynn said, smoothing his polo shirt as best he could, "starting tomorrow. It's too late for me to get a replacement from Timmons at this hour . . . Laura will be leaving for the theater in five or ten minutes."

Simone forced himself back to the conversation that had been interrupted by Andy. "She really hasn't had any problems with paparazzi or anything, Mr. Wynn. She can get by without me, I'm sure. . . ."

"No." The light blue eyes gripped Simone almost hypnotically; there was something urgent, even desperate, under Wynn's request. "I can tell she's upset, today, and you said yourself that last night turned ugly. It's just that kind of emotional state of affairs that could send her reeling."

"Mr. Wynn, if she takes a drink, I can't stop her—"

"But you'll be there to keep things in check. You'll be there to drive her, if nothing else. Damage control."

"Has she been drinking today?"

"No, no, no. No sign of that, but tonight, with her actor friends all round . . . Please. If you consent, I'll forget about this little scene with your partner. . . . I would imagine he would be in no small parcel of trouble, were I to report his presence here tonight, much less his behavior."

Simone sighed. Reluctantly nodded. "Just tonight, then."

Wynn smiled; even rich guys could still savor the pleasure of getting their own way, it seemed.

"Thank you, Detective Simone. Your partner has quite a temper."

"Yes he does. And if you did hire those contract

boys, I'd suggest you do as Andy says, and call them off. He'll keep his word about killing your ass."

Wynn's smile was nervous, and sickly. "I thought maybe that was, uh . . . at least partly bluster."

"He loves his wife, Mr. Wynn. You can understand the sorrow he'd feel if something happened to her— right? I'll just wait in the foyer."

And he left Wynn standing there, with hollow eyes and a slack jaw and knees gone so weak he was bracing himself against the blond desk.

TWELVE

In the long, narrow overgrown closet that was the detective squad's witness observation area, Sipowicz stood looking through the two-way mirror into Interview Two where sat the man in black, Leonard Parsons, leaning an elbow on the table and a hand on his face.

Next to Sipowicz at left was Sylvia, and Greg and Diane were at his right. Sipowicz had been beeped in the car, on his way home from Wynn's; he was still in a state of shock and outrage and hurt and bewilderment, from what he viewed as Bobby's betrayal. At the stationhouse he'd been met by Sylvia and the two detectives, who had shuttled him into this chamber for a quick I.D. On the way Diane gave him a capsule rundown on the capture, but did not get into what they'd learned from questioning the witness, wanting a cold identification from Andy.

"Is that him?" Greg asked. "Is that the guy?"

"No," Sipowicz said dryly, "it's Johnny freakin' Cash. Of course it's the guy. . . . Has he lawyered up?"

"An attorney's on the way," Sylvia said, adding

with a lilt in her voice, "An old friend, one James Sinclair."

Sipowicz frowned.

They all knew what that name meant: Sinclair was heavily mobbed up.

"Just don't try to tell me Giardella's behind this," Sipowicz said, his voice heavy with disbelief.

"That's the name Parsons gave us," Diane said. "That's the name of his employer."

"What, I suppose Alfonse is reachin' from beyond the grave, wearin' the haunted wig from hell?" Sipowicz shook his head, jerking a thumb toward the glass and the seated hitman. "Don't try to tell me the yuppie second cousin, with the designer threads, sent *this* guy? That kid has no reason—"

"Not Alfonse Giardella," Sylvia said, touching her husband's arm, "and not Angelo. Marianna Giardella."

"Who the fuck is that?"

"*Mrs.* Alfonse Giardella," Diane said.

Sipowicz felt like he'd been hit with a wet rag. "Mrs. Giardella," he said.

"The loving widow," Sylvia said.

"Jesus," Sipowicz said. "Why?"

Sylvia's laugh was short and bittersweet. "You think you're the only person on earth who likes to get even, Andy?"

Sipowicz, trying to absorb and process this news, heard himself asking, "This mope gave her up?"

"Yes," Diane said, nodding toward Parsons. "And admitted you were the intended victim."

Greg said, "He's reluctant to g-give up his partner. We haven't got that name as yet."

Diane said, "They're an item, Leonard and his partner."

"An item?" Sipowicz blinked. "You mean, ridin' the Hershey Highway type item?"

Diane nodded.

"When I dangled immunity in front of him, for his partner," Sylvia said, "Leonard got suddenly interested. He wants to discuss that with his attorney."

Sipowicz's eyes widened and he jerked a thumb toward the unknowing Parsons. "Sylvia—you didn't offer the gay caballero, here, immunity, did you?"

Patiently, firmly, Sylvia said, "How else do you think we could have gotten him to roll over on his employer?"

Sipowicz began to pace and gesture, as best he could in the cramped space. "That's not right, Sylvia. He busted in our place. He shot holes in our freakin' walls, he was gonna kill me, and I lost two goddamn good fish 'cause of that mutt. . . ."

"His reluctance to complete doing business with us," Sylvia said, with a twinkle in her eyes, "may benefit us in that regard."

Sipowicz stopped pacing, stood flatfooted. "Speak English."

She continued: "Holding out for a deal until his partner is included, and his attorney gets here to finalize details, and yet handing us that information in the meantime, gives us . . . what's the word, Andy?"

"Straddle," he said, a tiny knowing smile forming. "You decide you don't wanna prosecute Mrs. Giardella, and suddenly you don't need Leonard's testimony, and Leonard goes away on home invasion, ADW, and assorted goodies."

"Exactly," Sylvia said. "And if the state of Mrs. Giardella's health is as we understand it to be, not prosecuting is a definite possibility."

"James told us," Greg explained to Sipowicz, "what Angelo Giardella told you about Mrs. Giardella. That she is quite ill and hospitalized."

"Suffered several strokes, yeah," Sipowicz said. "What's James doin' around, after shift?"

"James and Adrianne were in on the La Paella collar," Diane said. "James is on the phone right now, calling hospitals, trying to find out where Mrs. Giardella is."

Sipowicz was studying the moon-faced mustached Parsons, as if viewing a distorted reflection of himself.

"Give me a couple minutes with him," Sipowicz said, "before his lawyer gets here."

"Andy," Sylvia said, and her voice had an edge, "I won't have you beating that man. You'll only taint our case—"

"Hey, you're gonna give him a free ride, anyway. What's the difference?"

"Fancy wouldn't go for this," Greg said.

"Fancy ain't here," Sipowicz said.

Sylvia touched his arm; her eyes pleaded with him. "Andy . . ."

Diane said, "This isn't such a great idea, Andy."

He smiled an easygoing smile that wasn't fooling anybody. "I ain't gonna muss a hair on his bald head.

I think I can get his partner's name out of him, is all. Once Sinclair gets here, that guy's gonna clam on us."

Soon, Greg was stepping into Interview Two, with Sipowicz following.

"Detective Sipowicz would like a few words with you," Greg said pleasantly, as Sipowicz took off his watch and handed that and his gun to Medavoy.

"No," Parsons said, scooting back in his chair, "no way! You can't leave me in here with—"

That was when Greg shut the door on them.

"So," Sipowicz said, smiling an awful smile, pulling out the chair nearest Parsons and placing his foot on the seat, then leaning forward on his knee. "We meet again."

The small dead eyes were blinking in the round pasty face. "I got nothing to say till my lawyer gets here."

"Don't you remember me, Leonard? We met at the dance last Sunday night. Remember waltzin' around with me?"

Parsons offered up a small, feeble smile. "Go ahead. Slap me around. You think I haven't taken a beating before? Consider this an invitation. It'll be my ticket outta here."

Sipowicz made a disappointed face. "You got me all wrong, Leonard. I'm grateful to you. You been cooperating real good, I hear, givin' up all sorts of names—including mine."

"I got nothing to say."

Now Sipowicz smiled. "Makes you kinda . . .

nervous . . . talkin' to one of your intended victims, does it?"

"Go ahead. Rough me up. I want you to."

"It must be kind of . . . embarrassing. I mean, it's nothin' personal, right? Just a job."

"I got nothing to say."

Sipowicz's hands were folded on the knee he leaned on. "I know we're not gonna be great friends, Leonard. It's just not meant to be. We come from different walks of life, you and me. You, you're in a violent kind of business. Me, I'm what you call a peace officer."

And Sipowicz grabbed Parsons and threw him into the wire-mesh outer wall of the holding cell. It didn't hurt Parsons much, but it startled hell out of him and made an awful racket, shaking, clattering. Then Parsons was pinned there, like a bug in a spider's web, as Sipowicz faced him, pushing a hand against his chest, the wall of mesh behind Parsons giving some.

"See, I just found out they're gonna give you immunity," Sipowicz said, showing his teeth but not smiling, anymore. "I just found out the guy that come in my place and was gonna whack me and maybe my wife—'cause you don't leave witnesses behind, do you, Leonard, not on no murder job—I just found out that you're gonna walk anyway, so I might as well get my two cents in with you while I got the chance."

The dead little eyes with alive with fear. "What do you want from me?"

"The name of your partner."

His brow furrowed. "No way."

"He'll get a free ride, too, Leonard."

"I'm waitin' for my lawyer!"

"I would just hate for your . . . friend . . . to, you know, get spooked when you don't show up tonight, and take off, and then suddenly he's a fugitive and you know fugitives have this tendency to get shot, Leonard, and we wouldn't want your main squeeze gettin' squooze, now would we?"

"No fucking way I'm telling you anything!"

Sipowicz was smiling the awful smile again. "We'll see about that, Leonard—"

The door opened and Sipowicz, still pinning the prisoner to the outer cage wall, glanced over his shoulder.

Fancy was standing there like a statue guarding the gate of an ancient city. He was wearing a dark blue windbreaker over a light blue shirt and gray slacks, and looked as casual as Sipowicz had ever seen the Loo look. He'd obviously been called at home, summoned to the precinct house because his people had made a major arrest.

But even so, there was nothing casual about the expression on Lt. Arthur Fancy's face.

"Andy," Fancy said, "a word?"

Sipowicz released the prisoner's shirt, and Parsons bounced against the wire-mesh cage a little.

"You're a very lucky man, Leonard," Sipowicz whispered. "Ed McMahon come to your house with a big freakin' check, you couldn't be no luckier."

In the hallway, Fancy said, "Do I have to say anything?"

Sipowicz avoided eye contact. "No, Loo."

That black carved mask that was Fancy's face gave nothing away; but the tone of his voice did: "I understand your emotions, here. You're a good cop, Andy, occasionally a great one. But I can't look the other way while you administer beatings to prisoners."

Sipowicz's mouth twitched. "I wasn't gonna beat him. I was usin' . . . psychology on him."

"I think you should go home. The case detectives are on this. I don't think they'll be needing your back-up."

"Okay, Loo."

Fancy nodded, and walked off.

Most of the 8-to-12 Tour detectives were out of the building, so James—who had noticed Sipowicz and Fancy's confab—was at his usual desk. He waved Sipowicz over.

"I got somethin'," James said. "I'm comin' to you with it first, Andy."

"What's that, kid?"

"Mrs. Giardella is at St. Luke's. I got the room number and everything."

Sipowicz had a quick look around; Fancy wasn't in sight, Sylvia either, nor Greg, nor Diane. "You, uh . . . wouldn't wanna come with me, James? And call on a sick acquaintance who I never met that wants me killed?"

James shrugged. "I'm up for that."

Heading down the stairs, they passed James Sinclair—fiftyish, cueball bald, distinguished, in a dark blue suit with silk deco-patterned tie, black leather briefcase in hand—and the attorney gave Sipowicz a look that was like a knife stab.

"And a pleasant good evening to you, counselor," Sipowicz said.

"Detective," Sinclair said musically, turning the one word into a cantata of contempt.

As Sinclair disappeared up into the squadroom, James said, "I don't think he likes you, Andy."

"Wait till he talks to his client," Sipowicz said. "I'm gonna zoom right up his hit parade."

Downstairs, the catching bench filled with junkies, whores, and other prime examples of humanity, Sipowicz signed out an unmarked car, collecting the keys from the 8-to-12 Tour desk sergeant, who said, "Little late for you, isn't it, detective?"

"Never too late," Sipowicz said, "to call on a sick friend."

THIRTEEN

Shortly after Andy Sipowicz had unceremoniously exited the Wynn penthouse, bodyguard Simone found himself again in the marble foyer beneath the glittering chandelier, waiting for his charge—in this case, an explosive charge.

Laura Wynn, in her uniform of black turtleneck and jeans and clunky boots, tromped down the curving staircase like a storm trooper into battle. Her face was a cold mask, though the spooky light blue eyes were burning.

With a smile that was more a sneer, she said to Simone, "Fasten your seat belt—it's going to be a bumpy night."

That was a movie or play reference, Simone realized, but he couldn't recall what from.

"I was out of line last night," he said.

"Is that an apology?"

"I let things get too personal. It was unprofessional."

That wasn't what she wanted to hear. "You're a prick, Simone."

And they didn't speak again until halfway down

Broadway, in the rental Taurus. She was staring out the window at nothing, arms folded, the neon reflecting on her features, colors shifting in waves.

Normally Simone wouldn't have said anything; but he was churning inside over Andy going off on him, and she was getting to him, this self-centered, incredibly spoiled brat.

"I'd think you'd learn to deal with it by now, in your line of work," he said.

She glared at him. "Deal with what?"

"Rejection."

Her eyes flared, nostrils too, and she flung herself at him (as far as her seat belt would allow, anyway), and began beating on him, pummeling him with small hard fists, and he veered into the next lane, getting honked and sworn at. He shoved her aside and she bounced against the passenger's side window and then slumped in her seat and covered her face with both hands and wept.

"Nutcase," he said.

She began to sob.

Was this a performance? Or was the young actress's life filled with dramatic scenes like this, over the top and yet very real?

She snuffled. "You . . . you think I don't . . . don't have *feelings*? You think I don't miss my mother?"

What brought that *on*?

"You lost your wife . . . you should understand how . . . how emotionally vulnerable I am right now."

Tears on her cheeks glistened in the reflection of blue and red and yellow neon gliding by.

"I'm sorry," he said, and he was. She was right: he had behaved like a prick. Or was that a role she had forced him into?

"Pull over," she ordered.

"Where?"

"Up there."

The red sign said LIQUOR—24 HOURS.

She pointed. "There's a loading zone you can pull into."

"I don't think so."

She glowered at him. "Pull over, Simone. You're the hired help, remember? You just work here."

"I work for your father."

Her smile was brittle. "I just want to get some cigarettes, and some Kleenex, to fix my face up so I'm not further humiliated when my fellow actors get a look at me under the lights, when I get made up."

Tonight was dress rehearsal for "The Star-Wagon."

Simone pulled over, and she quickly got out. A few minutes later she returned with a brown grocery sack that clinked with glass as she placed it on the floor between her legs.

"You lied," he said.

"No I didn't, she said, and reached into the sack and brought out a pack of Virginia Slims and a small purse-size Kleenex package. But he glimpsed the screw-on caps of three liquor bottles as well.

"Don't do it," he said.

She lit up a Virginia Slim, blew out smoke. "Do what?"

"I'm not worth falling off the wagon for."

"Film at eleven."

"Please, Laura.

She arched an eyebrow. "Oh, you *do* care about me?"

He leaned closer. "Yeah. Yeah, I do."

That seemed to melt her again, and her voice mingled warmth with hurt as she said, "You got a funny way of showing it."

She wanted him to kiss her, but it didn't feel right to him, though she really was lovely, even with runny mascara and smudged lipstick.

"Maybe we can talk later," he said, pulling out into a hole in the traffic. "Right now you've got work to do."

She nodded, smiled bravely, and put on her minimal mascara and lipstick, using the mirrored light on the visor.

The "tech" dress rehearsal, as Laura referred to it, meaning full makeup, wardrobe, lighting, even music cues, went very well. Simone—even though sitting through the play for what was the third time in as many days—got caught up in it. The period dress seemed to inspire the actors, and bring the story alive. Laura was particularly good, believable and sympathetic both as the older version of the character (the nagging wife) and the younger (the encouraging sweetheart).

The director's notes were quick and upbeat, and by eleven, an almost giddy Laura came streaming up the aisle to Simone's seat near the back, all the makeup scrubbed from her face, looking about twelve, blond hair down and bouncing off her shoulders, light blue eyes glittering.

"It was good, wasn't it? I mean, really good."

"Yes," Simone said.

"You're not just saying that."

"No."

"Goody goody goody!"

He found her childish glee rather charming, but also a little neurotic.

She looped her arm in his. "Guy and Larry and Sarah are going over to Shakespeare's."

"Not familiar with it."

"It's in the West Village—I'll point the way."

On the drive over, she re-applied her makeup in the visor mirror and said, "Tomorrow's the invited dress rehearsal."

"What's that?"

"It's like tonight, only with an audience. They're warned by the director, at the top of the show, that it's a rehearsal and we might have to stop . . . but you never do. You won't need a ticket till Friday night."

His hands tightened on the wheel. "Laura . . . I won't be with you tomorrow night, or Friday."

She put her lipstick away. "Why? Some conflict?"

"No. . . . This is my last night."

"What? What are you talking about?"

"I told your father, before you came down."

Her eyes were saucers. "You mean, you *quit*?"

"Yes. I only came on tonight because it was too late to get a replacement."

Her upper lip curled. "Oh, you mean I'm that loathsome?"

"Of course not . . . damnit, does everything have to be a scene with you?"

"My father knew you were quitting and he didn't say anything to me?"

"I don't think he had the chance—"

"Yes he did. He came upstairs and wished me break-a-leg. He could have told me."

Simone shrugged. "Maybe he didn't want to upset you."

She folded her arms and stared straight ahead, into nothing. "Why should it upset me if some Puerto Rican off-duty cop doesn't want to spend time with me?"

"Laura. . . ."

Now an exchange began between them that—for anyone in the next lane who might notice the argument in progress—would seem a study in extremes: the stoic male at the wheel, occasionally punctuating his words by tossing a glance at the animated female who sat sideways in the rider's seat, staring him down with wild, accusing eyes.

"Why did you quit?"

"Like I said earlier . . . it wasn't professional. . . ."

"Do you take pleasure in humiliating me?"

"Everything isn't about you."

"What?"

"You think you're starring in the story of your life, and the rest of us are bit players. There are other things going on in the world besides the story of you, Laura."

"Long speech for a bit player."

"I quit because I *do* like you—and I felt bad."

"Bad? Why bad?"

"I didn't like my motives."

Sarcasm twisted her pretty features. "What, are we back to you feeling guilty for French-Portuguese kissing me?"

"I took this job to get next to you . . . not to get over on you, beautiful as you are, but to . . . to try to get something on your father."

"What does *he* have to with anything?"

Simone braced himself, and told her: "My partner is married to the assistant district attorney who prosecuted your father."

Her eyes widened, filled with pain, then with rage. Her fists were ready to pummel him again, but somehow she managed to restrain her actions.

But not her words, and a flurry of obscenities labeling him in various unflattering ways ended with: "You . . . bastard! You were using me, pumping me for information!"

"I just took the job your father offered. He knew who I was."

Now her eyes narrowed, brimming with unpleasant surprise. "He knew who you were? He knew you were investigating my mother's murder, and he still hired you?"

"Yes."

She shook her head, breathing hard, as if winded from a long, losing race. "I don't know who's sicker . . . you or him. As far as I'm concerned, you can both go to hell."

And she turned away from him, staring out the window.

Soon they were in Shakespeare's, a burgers-and-brews actor's hangout with the expected Elizabethan theme, whitewashed wood, wooden booths, a large one of which played host to the group from *The Star-Wagon.*

"Here's to us," Guy Hamilton said, lifting his Scotch on the rocks. The soap opera actor—whose short, well-groomed brown hair and generally clean-cut look made his tattered gray sweatshirt seem an affectation—was already on his second drink. "We've taken a cornball old vehicle, and ridden it to the stars!"

"Here's to us," Larry Philborne agreed, and lifted his glass of wine. Larry, the play's pudgy comedy relief, wore a *Comedy Relief* football jersey.

Sarah Walker joined in, lifting her Miller Lite; she was in her mid-twenties, a busty, attractive if anorexic brunette in a big dark-green sweater (she played the boss's daughter in the play, the largest female role next to Laura's). As was the case with many actresses, Sarah's features—which from the audience seemed extremely pretty—appeared rather exaggerated up close.

Simone was getting a good look, because he was seated by the wall, next to her, Laura having squeezed in next to Guy and Larry on the other side of the booth.

"To us," Laura said, and instead of drinking from her own 7-Up, she borrowed Guy's tumbler of Scotch and took a hefty swig. She held it in her mouth, savoring it, looking at Simone as she did, as if daring him to stop her—then she swallowed.

"Don't," Simone said quietly.

She gave him a tiny smile and raised her eyebrows,

creating an expression that was at once defiant and arrogant.

"Little girls' room," she said, and scooted out of the booth.

Guy was watching her go, with some concern. "Say, uh, Bobby—I thought little Laura was off the sauce."

"She is," Simone said.

"Or was," Sarah said.

"I heard Betty Ford," Larry said.

"You heard right," Simone said. "Maybe we should break this up, if you don't mind . . . or you might have a problem, tomorrow night, when the curtain goes up."

"And, jeez, we've been drinking around her, all along," Larry said. "I mean, I thought she was comfortable with that."

"This isn't about you people drinking," Simone said. "It's about her drinking."

"And whatever demons drive her," Guy said.

Did all these actors view life as some ongoing melodrama?

"I haven't got my salad yet," Sarah said.

Guy and Larry had burgers coming, so the consensus was, no more drinks, and after the food, the party would be over.

Laura sauntered up, and she had her own double Scotch on the rocks in hand, which was already half gone.

So was she.

"Did I miss anything interesting?" Her eyes were bright and dull at the same time. "Little Sarah here put a knife in my back yet? Larry go down on Guy, under the booth? Anything cute or fun?"

Embarrassed, worried glances were exchanged by her companions, as Laura again pushed in on Guy's side.

"We're going to cut this short, dear," Guy said pleasantly, though the blood had drained out of his face, probably due to his unease at seeing Dr. Jekyll disappear and Ms. Hyde show up. "We're going to eat and run—want to be fresh for tomorrow."

Laura had finished her double Scotch and was waving for another. "Then might I suggest you not stay up all night, banging your untalented paramour?"

"That's cruel," Larry said. He, too, had lost the blood in his face and his eyes might have been tearing up.

The food arrived (burgers all around except for Sarah's salad), and Laura handed her empty glass to the waitress, instructed her on what to fill it with, and said carefully to Larry, "Let me tell you what's cruel . . . Laurence. What's cruel is to expose an audience to an acting style that makes 'Gilligan's Island' seem subtle by comparison."

"We're not exactly performing Strindberg, dear," Guy said testily.

"And you're so much more brilliant than Maxwell fucking Anderson, who only wrote *The Bad Seed* and *What Price Glory?*" She leaned so close to Guy their noses almost touched. "And how do you spend the days of *your* lives, 'dear'? Playing butch on 'The Young and the Dickless'!"

Sarah, who'd been picking at her salad awkwardly,

pushed the bowl aside and said, "I, uh, think I better go . . ."

Laura's eyes were like ice-blue lasers again, only not so pleasant, tonight; she trained them on the actress. "May I give you a little beauty tip, darling? If you're going to starve yourself to death, buy smaller boobs. You look grotesque."

"I won't put up with this," Sarah said, face clenching like a fish, "even if your father *is* backing the goddamn show . . ."

Now it was Laura's face that drained of blood. "What?"

Guy and Larry exchanged "oh shit" glances.

Sarah looked away. "Nothing. Excuse me." She slid out of the booth, but Laura grabbed her by the arm. Tight.

"What are you talking about, you skinny little talentless bitch?" Laura's lips were peeled back over her teeth. "My father has nothing to do with this production!"

No one said anything.

Sarah pulled loose and scurried away, her legs in the black leggings under the bulky sweater like knitting needles carrying away a big green ball of yarn.

"My father doesn't have anything to do with this . . ." Laura glared accusingly at Guy. "*Does* he?"

"He's the prime angel, yes," Guy said, with urbane resignation. "We were told not to say anything. But you charmed it out of us. Excuse me. Ex-*cuse* me?"

Sneering, Laura stepped out of the booth and let the two actors out. Guy snatched up the check and

Larry flashed her a hurt look and then they were gone.

Sitting opposite Simone, she finished off her Scotch, then shot the blue laser beams across the booth at him. "Did you know anything about that?" Laura demanded.

"About what?"

"My father backing the show."

"No."

"That bastard. That lousy bastard . . ." She grabbed a passing waitress by the arm.

"Hey!" the waitress said, and Laura thrust the glass at the young woman, a startled redhead who was probably an actress herself but one who didn't have a father to back her play, anonymously or otherwise.

"Scotch rocks, double," Laura spat.

"Okay!" the waitress said, wide-eyed, and muttered the word "Bitch," under her breath.

Laura fixed the lasers on him, again. "You didn't know? You really didn't know?"

"No."

She looked down at her hands folded before her. "Bastard."

"Why is he a bastard for helping out his daughter?"

Her chin crinkled; she was crying. "He shouldn't have lied to me."

"Maybe he just wanted you to feel good about yourself.

"Yeah, and aren't I just basking in high self-fucking-esteem!"

"You don't need that Scotch. Let's go. Right now."

"You work for *me*, asshole!"

"We're going." He got out of the booth. "Come on."

She looked at him with her teeth showing; it was like having a leopard get ready to snarl at you. "Put a hand on me and see what happens."

"You want to find your own way home?"

Suddenly she got teary-eyed again. "No. No. Bobby . . . don't leave . . ."

"Then behave. And skip that next drink."

She swallowed, contrite. "Okay. Okay . . ."

He escorted her out of there and in the car, on the way back to Central Park West, she wept. Sobbing; heaving racking sobs.

In the parking garage of the apartment building, Simone said, "I'll walk you up."

"Okay."

But she reached down to the front-seat floor and gathered up in her arms the brown paper sack with the bottles of booze in it.

"No," Simone said. "Leave that behind."

"The hell," she said, with the snarling expression.

And she got out of the car. He followed her to the elevator and she clutched that sack to her bosom as if it were her lifeline. They went up to the lobby, changed elevators, silent all the way. At the door to the penthouse, she paused.

"Will you come in?" she asked.

"Leave the sack out here and I'll come in."

"If I do, will you come upstairs?"

"I don't think so."

She sneered. "Prick."

The evening had come full circle.

He sighed and used the key, pushed open the door for her. Her father, silver-haired, tanned, wearing a belted canary-yellow bathrobe, was waiting in the foyer; he must have heard them in the hall.

"Are you all right . . . ?" he began, but then he saw his daughter, saw her disheveled state and smelled the booze on her and noted the paper bag in her arms, making its telltale glass clink as she hugged it to her.

"Simone," Wynn said, his face a ghastly white, "I'm disappointed in you."

"Not in *me*?" she asked her father. "You bastard . . . you miserable bastard."

She placed the bag ever so gently in an antique white chair beneath a fresco of floating angels, and flew at her father with those pummeling fists.

Simone began to pull her away from Wynn, but Wynn clutched his daughter to his breast even as she pummeled him, weeping, and the father said to the detective, "Please leave us!"

Somehow, sobs catching in her throat, she pulled out of her father's arms, snatched up the sack of clinking bottles, and ran up the stairs as if she were fleeing some demon, inner or otherwise.

Wynn looked up the curving stairs at the door slamming; oddly, it was the door to the pink bedroom, the child's room, not the guest room where she said she slept.

"Oh Christ," Wynn said.

"Is there anything I can do?"

Wynn frowned. "No. You've done quite enough."

Simone returned the frown. "Hey, I did my best. I told you, if she started to drink, there was no way I could stop her—she's an adult."

"Technically," he sighed. He shook his head. "It's not your fault. If anything, it's mine."

"You going to be all right?"

"I think so."

"You'll get her help?"

"Of course. Tomorrow."

"Is there somebody you can call tonight? Her aunt maybe? I know she's close to her."

"Yes. You're right." Wynn held up a hand, in a stop gesture. "Please go, Mr. Simone. This is a family matter, now."

"You're sure there's nothing—"

"Please go."

Simone swallowed thickly. "If that's what you want, sir."

"It's what I want."

"You understand I'm speaking not as your employee, but as a police officer—"

"I do."

Reluctantly, feeling at least as helpless as Wynn must have, Simone left the penthouse.

FOURTEEN

Midnight at St. Luke's Roosevelt Hospital was way past time for visitors. But Andy Sipowicz and James Martinez, badges on their lapels, went up the elevator to Intensive Care and walked down the darkened corridor, without anyone saying a word. The place seemed fairly deserted, save for the lit-up nurses' stations where the detectives passed by unnoticed or at least unremarked upon. Nurses' aides shuffled along with the glazed expressions that accompanied thankless underpaying jobs; women of various ethnic backgrounds who didn't look very fit for working in the health-care profession. The detectives' footsteps joined the occasional coughs, the heartbeat-monitor blips, and the slaps of a janitor's mop, sounds that stood out in this quiet world.

As they approached her room, they found Mrs. Giardella's door open; the lights were out.

"Wait here, I'll check it out," Sipowicz said to James, stepping inside. A cracked door to the bathroom revealed a light was left on; that, and a little light from the corridor, guided him to her bed (the only bed in the room—the Giardellas could afford privacy) where she lay with tubes running in and out of her—her nose, her arms, hanging bags of fluid next to the bed, a flatline monitor blipping along, a digital monitor showing her blood pressure rate.

Sipowicz switched on the light over the bed, a reading light really, and it didn't disturb her. She continued sleeping, a thin withered woman with a witch's nose amid otherwise pleasant features grown haggard with illness, her flesh as gray as cigarette smoke, her hair a sickly gray-white. She was rather tall, judging by the bony form visible under the white sheet. She could have been seventy-five, though it was his understanding that Giardella's wife was in her early fifties. Like Giardella had been, before his dago pals snuffed him in that FBI-funded hotel suite.

Sipowicz went to the door, started to close himself in, saying to James, "You mind?"

"Naw," the kid said, folding his arms, positioning himself with his back to the wall.

Door shut, Sipowicz went back to the bed and looked down at this frail woman, a woman he'd never seen before, and he gently nudged her, hoping they didn't have her so doped up on sleeping pills that his mission was hopeless.

Her eyes opened suddenly, startling him, like a corpse's eyes opening in a horror movie.

Oddly, they were very beautiful eyes, a deep blue, and long-lashed; unfortunately, they were buried in deep sockets.

The eyes narrowed. "Who . . . who . . ."

"You ought to know the face of the man you want dead, Mrs. Giardella."

And she recognized him, eyes widening, the heart-beat blips accelerating, the blood-pressure gauge dancing digitally.

"You . . . bastard . . ." she said.

"I never done nothing to you, lady. It was all between me and your husband."

"I . . . I loved my . . . husband."

"Well, a dirty job but somebody had to do it."

"Al . . . Al is dead . . . because of you. . . ."

Weak as her voice was, the hatred in it was strong.

Sipowicz said, "He's dead because he rolled over on the boys."

"You . . . you drove him . . . drove him . . . pushed him to those . . . those bad decisions. . . ."

"The guy you hired, Leonard Parsons? He's made of the same stuff as your late husband. What I mean to say is, he's rolled over on you, lady. Gave you up."

"Son of . . . son of a bitch . . ."

"You talkin' about Parsons, or me? Oh, well. It don't matter. I just wanted to wish you, get well soon . . . so you can go away on conspiracy to commit murder."

"Go . . . go to hell. . . ."

"You seem a little hostile. Maybe next time I'll bring flowers and candy. Perk you right up."

"What . . . what do you . . . want from me?"

"I don't suppose you'd give me the name of the other button guy? Leonard's pal?"

"Fuh . . . fuck you."

"I didn't think so. You get some rest. Try not to overdo okay?"

She spewed some obscenities in a language that was either Italian or Sicilian—Andy wasn't sure—but it did put a smile on his face as he left there, leaving the reading light on.

He stepped out of the room and James said, "Well?"

"She took the contract out all right."

"Get anything else out of her?"

"I think she tried to give me a recipe for cannolis there, at the end."

James frowned. "You think she's dyin'?"

"I hope so."

Sipowicz had barely got that out when, from around the corner, walking quickly, and even at midnight looking like a fashion model in a gray pinstripe suit with a light gray turtleneck, came Angelo Giardella, Italian heels clicking, echoing like tiny firecrackers.

"It's a little after visiting hours, isn't it, Detective?" the young Giardella asked, eyes hard and alert behind the gold-frame glasses, arms folded, planting himself before Sipowicz.

"Same back at ya, Angelo," Sipowicz said. "What brings you around at this time of night to see . . . what is she to you, anyway? She's not your aunt. Your second cousin's wife, what is that called, anyway?"

"She's a very sick woman."

"Yeah, she needs a psychiatrist, all right. And she's lookin' a little run-down, to boot."

"You're a cruel man, Detective Sipowicz."

Sipowicz pointed toward the room. "Your relation

in there tried to have me killed. In fact, one of the two men she hired is still at large, putting me and my wife in current danger, so don't expect much compassion from me for the crazy mafia wife who put this whole merry-go-round in motion. She's lucky I didn't smother her with a pillow."

James asked, "How *do* you happen to be dropping by the hospital this time of night, Mr. Giardella?"

The young pornography mogul seemed suddenly nervous. "I'm not sure that's any of your business."

Sipowicz said, "It couldn't have been James Sinclair that called him, James, 'cause that would be a betrayal of Sinclair's client, Leonard Parsons. I mean, Sinclair would have to be a real sleazebag to call Angelo here when he found out his client was rolling over on Mrs. G."

"Yeah," James said, "that would be violation of attorney/client ethics or something."

"The bar association definitely ought to hear about this," Sipowicz said.

"Look," Angelo said. "I know you're upset—"

"Naw," Sipowicz said. "These things happen. People hire people to kill people all the friggin' time. Particularly in a slimy business like yours, Angelo."

Young Giardella held up his palm in a gesture of reason. "I want you to know that I . . . had no knowledge of what Mrs. Giardella did."

Sipowicz thought about that. "You mean, you're sayin' she acted on her own."

"Independently," Angelo said. "Without any approval from any, uh, authority."

Meaning, it wasn't a mob-sanctioned hit.

Sipowicz, relieved to hear that, said, "I guess, she would know what phone calls to make, to line up somebody like Parsons."

Angelo nodded. "She was intimately involved in the business. She had been Alfonse's secretary, before they were married, and she remained his close business associate till the very end."

"The second guy is still out there," Sipowicz said. "Parsons' partner, and soul mate. Parsons may give him up by tomorrow, but he might also, through Sinclair, get word to him to scram."

Angelo shrugged. "I can't promise you that I can convince Mrs. Giardella to give me that name. She's dying, Detective Sipowicz. She has no reason to cooperate . . . but she also is in no position to cause any further trouble."

"Yeah. I can see that."

"As for Leonard Parsons, this is a little out of my area, but I'm sure that there are those who will not appreciate Parsons betraying Mrs. Giardella."

Sipowicz studied the handsome face, carefully, keeping in mind the close-set eyes were those of Alfonse Giardella. "You mean, just because she was workin' on her own devices, that don't mean you want some button guy rollin' over on her to the D.A.'s office."

"Correct. She may be misguided, but she's still part of the family."

"So, then, uh, I shouldn't be too concerned, should this Parsons take a walk on this thing."

"No. I would say there's every reason to expect

that that score will be settled, by my associates, in their own way, and their own time."

"I can live with that," Sipowicz said. "You latch on to Parsons' partner's name and/or whereabouts, drop a dime, okay?"

"You have my word."

"I wish I had a copy of Larry Flynt's autobiography, for you to swear on," Sipowicz said.

Then he nodded to James and they started down the hall.

"I'll just see how Mrs. Giardella is doing," Angelo said.

"You do that," Sipowicz said. "And keep your nose clean, kid—you don't wanna get on my bad side."

"No I don't," young Giardella said, and he stepped in the hospital room of his second cousin's widow.

On the way over, in the car, Sipowicz had told James about Bobby's betrayal. It had been a full-scale rave-out and James had kept quiet.

Now, in the car again, on the way back to the stationhouse, James said, "You know, you were wrong about that Wynn character. This thing had nothin' to do with him."

Sipowicz was behind the wheel. He looked over at James like the kid had passed gas. "Yeah. So?"

James lifted his eyebrows, shrugged. "So, maybe you oughta lighten up on Bobby. I mean, have you even heard his side of it?"

Anger flushed Andy's face. "Hey, there ain't no side of it that's worth hearing. He was supposed to be my friend, my partner, and he takes a job workin' for that gold karat slimeball?"

"Wynn didn't take out the contract, Andy—"

"Bobby didn't know that! No, he let me down. He went way around the bend, way outta line on this one. Tomorrow, I ask Fancy for a new partner. I've fuckin' had it."

"You gotta hear him out, Andy," James said.

Sipowicz grunted, cursed at a cabbie who pulled in front of him.

"Life is too short to throw away your friends, man," James said. "You wanna wind up in bed, like Mrs. G? Lettin' the hate eat you to death, from inside?"

Sipowicz didn't reply. He just drove, and cursed at stupid drivers.

FIFTEEN

Simone felt odd, coming into the stationhouse at this time of night; but when Diane summoned him (he'd been in the elevator, coming down from the Wynn penthouse, when his beeper beeped), he knew it had to be serious. Crossing that mutual distance they'd put between each other couldn't have been easy for her.

She looked tired yet alert, as she gestured him into the locker room for a private conference. Quickly, she filled him in on the events of the evening: the arrest of Parsons, the deal Sylvia had cut with the prisoner, the information Parsons had given up, as well as Andy's "interrogation" of the prisoner, which Fancy himself had interrupted. Things were really popping, Simone thought, especially considering their regular shift had been over for something like eight hours.

"Andy and James took off somewhere," she said. "I think Andy may be getting himself into some difficulty."

"What makes you think that?"

"James was checking hospitals to see where Mrs. Giardella was staying."

"And you think James came up with it? And went to Andy first?"

Diane nodded. "But do you think Andy could've convinced James to go along with him, to wherever she's being hospitalized?"

Simone twitched a humorless smirk. "Yeah. James would go along with that, coming from Andy."

"Andy seemed . . . he seemed wired, even for Andy."

He sighed. "Yeah, and I think I know why."

"Yeah?"

And he told her what had been going on with Wynn, and how Andy had barged in there earlier tonight, and had gotten the wrong idea.

Her brow was tight with confusion and concern. "Why didn't you straighten him out?"

"He didn't give me a chance, and anyway, I was kind of in shock. That he'd think that of me."

Her smile was warm, yet a little patronizing. "Bobby . . . Andy's an alcoholic."

"What does that have to do with anything? He isn't drinking—"

"No. But he's still got the alcoholic's personality profile. And you know what a hothead he can be. He's capable of assuming the worst of anybody, even you, because his own self-esteem is so low."

He smiled at her. "You're awful wise, all of a sudden."

"Twelve Step program," she said with a wry little smirk. "Makes an expert out of you, one day at a time."

"So you are in AA?"

She nodded. "Andy's my sponsor."

"I thought AA frowned on opposite-sex sponsors."

"Usually. And they don't recommend a sponsor being somebody you work with, either. But Andy made it happen. He said it takes a cop to understand a cop. . . . He's been great, Bobby."

He frowned. "Does Sylvia know this?"

"No. Nobody outside the meetings knows, really. I haven't wanted to advertise my problem . . . I don't really want the brass finding out, y'know? Anyway, it's private. It's . . . personal. Really nobody else's business."

"Then why are you telling me?"

She thought about that, then admitted, "I don't know."

He touched her face. "I'm glad you did."

She beamed at him. "*I'm* glad I did."

He wanted to kiss her, but this was the locker room, and maybe he wasn't ready, anyway—and maybe she wasn't, either. She would have to tell him. He would wait.

He asked, "Is the Loo still in the house?"

"Yeah."

"What about Sylvia?"

"She's still here. Waiting on pins and needles for Andy to get back."

He scratched his chin. "I need to talk to her."

Sylvia was in Interview One, which was serving its secondary function: squadroom lounge. This was where the coffee maker and microwave and occasional roll could be found. Simone pulled up a chair

and smiled at Sylvia and she smiled back; both their
faces had seen better smiles.

"Don't worry," he told her. "Andy can take care
of himself."

"Sure he can," she said with half a smile. "He's
just full of common sense."

"He'll show up, soon. You'll see."

"I know." She arched an eyebrow. "The question
is, will he still have a job?"

Simone sighed, twitched his own half-smile. "I
need to talk to him. I threw him a bad curve,
tonight."

"What?"

He filled her in, briefly.

"I'm sorry he thought the worst of you, Bobby,"
she said, shaking her head. "I'd like to say that's not
like him . . . but he does have that capacity."

"Hey, a guy with Andy's strengths has a got a
right to a few weaknesses. Last time I looked, I
wasn't perfect."

"Close enough, as far as I'm concerned." She
shook her head again. "We've had a bad few days,
Andy and me."

"Sorry to hear that."

"I know it's crazy, but"—she lowered her voice—
"I'm finding myself starting to get jealous of Detective Russell. She calls him all the time, *at home*,
and—"

Simone touched her hand. "I think there's something you need to know."

He told her what Diane had told him.

Her expression was chagrined, and frustrated.

"Why couldn't Andy just tell me what this was about?"

"It's like Diane said . . . it's personal. It's a club they belong to that we don't."

"I feel like a fool."

Diane stuck her head in. "Am I interrupting? I just want to get a cup of coffee."

"Come on in," Simone said. "Matter of fact, sit down, after you get your coffee. I wouldn't mind you hearing this."

"Okay," Diane said, getting herself a cup, good and black.

Simone leaned forward and he spoke quietly. "Sylvia . . . I want to float a new theory past you, on the Victoria Wynn homicide. I got some new insights tonight . . . not very pleasant ones, but valuable."

"Go ahead."

With an expression that indicated he hardly believed he was saying this, Simone said, "I'm liking the daughter for the murder."

Sylvia's composure erupted in skepticism. "The *daughter*? She was out of the state! Not even the tabloids came up with—"

Simone patted the air. "Hear me out . . . Laura Wynn is a seriously disturbed young woman who had a stormy relationship with her mother. She's also an alcoholic, and a very nasty one. As beautiful as she is, that's how ugly a drunk she is."

The Assistant D.A.'s eyes were tight; so was her brow. "Capable of killing her own mother?"

He shrugged with his shoulder and his eyebrows. "She's violent, when she drinks. Suppose she killed her mother, in a drunken rage? With that carving knife, and nicked herself in the process? That might explain the DNA match-up, wouldn't it?"

Sylvia shifted in her chair; she was coming around. "I'm not a forensics expert, but it might at that."

Coffee cup in hand, Diane pulled up a chair and said, "Laura would appear to be a chip off her mother's block. When we talked to Constance Reed, she made it clear her sister was a heavy drinker, and physically abusive."

"So then," Sylvia said, "daughter may have killed mother in self-defense . . . it may have been *Laura Wynn* who was in the drunken rage."

"Or it may have been two violent, inebriated women going at it," Simone said, with another shrug. "In any case, I don't think it's a stretch to think that J. Michael Wynn would cover up what his daughter did."

"But if he lost his wife because of her . . ." Diane began.

"He didn't want to lose his daughter, too," Simone said. "So he buys an alibi from a boyfriend, placing Laura at one of the family getaways out of state. Then he gets her immediately into rehab, and forces her to move back home and begins controlling her life, monitoring her activities."

Diane asked him, "You think the aunt would be as inclined to protect Laura as her father would?"

He nodded. "Laura and her aunt were very close, but the aunt keeps her distance now; though from what I observed, they're joined by some mutual concern . . . or secret."

"So Wynn stood trial," Diane said, with a dawning smile, "knowing he and his legal 'dream team'—and that unshakable alibi from his sister-in-law—would get him off? That's your theory?"

Simone ventured one more shrug. "That's *a* theory. What do you think, Sylvia?"

"I think," she said, "I'm going to discuss it with Maury Abrams tomorrow."

"I just hope the District Attorney's office won't feel they'll get too much egg on their face," Simone said, "going after a different defendant in this case."

The sound of a throat clearing took their attention to the doorway where Andy Sipowicz stood, his eyes so darkly circled he looked like a haunted raccoon.

"Sylvia," he said, "you ready to call it a night?"

"No," she said, rising. Puzzled, Andy stepped into the room to let her pass. Then she added: "Not till you and Bobby talk."

And she and Diane left the two of them there.

SIXTEEN

As Sylvia shut the door on them, Sipowicz—wondering why he was feeling guilty when this thing was all Bobby's fault—sauntered over to the coffeemaker and got himself a cup. Simone was sitting at the interrogation table, in the chair usually taken by suspects, and he was staring at the tabletop as if its scarred surface held some secret meaning.

Stirring in some cream, Sipowicz—his back to Bobby—said, "Certain people around here think I oughta give you a chance to, you know . . . tell your side."

Bobby said nothing.

Sipowicz sipped the coffee, his back still to Bobby, looking at the bulletin board of wanted circulars. "Okay, then. We leave it like it was."

Bobby said nothing.

"I put in for a new partner, tomorrow," Sipowicz said. "If that's how you want it."

"Your call," Bobby said.

Sipowicz twitched a non-smile, nodded, shrugged, and headed for the door, coffee cup in hand.

He was halfway out when Bobby said, "I didn't earn the benefit of a moment's doubt, Andy?"

Sipowicz glared at Bobby, who was looking up at him with hooded dark eyes. "What's that supposed to mean?"

"The other guy—would you have jumped his case like that, without hearin' his story, first?"

Sipowicz frowned and his eyes moved side to side. "I was with him a lot of years."

Bobby's dark eyes again stared at the tabletop. "Yeah. I suppose. That would make a difference."

Sipowicz stepped back in, shut the door, almost slamming it. "I'm askin' for your story—now. I'm listenin'."

Bobby looked up; his expression was cool yet something burned behind it. "I took that job so I could poke around under Wynn's nose. He knew who I was and didn't mind—I think he had the half-assed idea he and his daughter could win me over."

Sipowicz snorted a humorless laugh. "Did they?"

"Wynn seems like a decent enough guy—"

"Decent guy!"

"—and his daughter is sweet . . . till she starts drinking. Then she turns certifiable."

Sipowicz was interested in spite of himself. "You're sayin' the daughter's missin' a few dots on her dominoes?"

Bobby's nod was slow, the dark eyes knowing. "She is one seriously whacked-out little rich girl."

Sipowicz listened intently as Bobby shared with him the theory that Laura Wynn might have killed her mother, albeit possibly in self-defense. Bobby gave a detailed account of what he'd observed, particularly tonight, and by mid-way through, Sipowicz had taken a seat, rubbing his chin in a gesture of nervous thought.

"Your better half thinks this has enough merit," Bobby said, "to discuss it with Abrams tomorrow."

Sipowicz, brow furrowed, was nodding. "I can see it, the daughter. It coulda gone down like that."

An uneasy silence hung in the room, like ground fog.

Bobby said, "I hear Leonard Parsons gave up his employer."

"*Mrs.* Giardella, ain't that a blast from the past." Sipowicz shook his head. "I just spent a charming few minutes with that broad. She's so fulla hate, she's like a boil about to burst. Jesus, Bobby, why didn't you just *tell* me?"

"You didn't give me a chance. You jumped my ass."

Sipowicz shook his head, frustrated. "I don't mean tonight. I mean, *before* tonight. Why didn't you tell me you had an inside track on Wynn?"

Bobby leaned forward, almost getting in Sipowicz's face. "Because just going anywhere *near* Wynn, I was disobeying a direct order from Fancy, remember? I didn't see any reason your job should be on the line, too. Besides, you really think you coulda controlled yourself, knowing I had that kind of access to Wynn?"

". . . I can control myself when I feel like it."

A single laugh came from deep in Bobby's chest. "You'd've had me loanin' you keys to search the penthouse, you'd been runnin' illegal bugs, I'd've been wearin' a wire, you'd've been wearin' a kell, or hidin' in the backseat. . . . It would've been the Marx Brothers with guns."

"Okay, okay. You make your point."

Bobby's mouth tightened momentarily, then without looking at Sipowicz, he said, "Situation was reversed, I wouldn'ta done that to you Andy. Jumped your shit like that."

For some reason Bobby acting hurt irritated Sipowicz, and he blustered, "Hey, yeah, well maybe you're a younger, better man than me. If you're waitin' for an apology, it ain't gonna happen."

Bobby glared at him. "What, are you waitin' for *me* to apologize? All right—I'm sorry my partner is an asshole."

Sipowicz took that with a blank face, then said, "I guess it's all right you call me that."

"What? 'Asshole'?"

Sipowicz grunted another laugh. "Everybody calls me that. I mean, 'partner.' This is one of them breakdowns in communication you hear so much about . . . nothin' worth breakin' up a good workin' relationship over. You think?"

"Naw." Bobby offered up a tiny shrug. "This current arrangement's fine."

Another silence settled on the room, but a much more comfortable one.

"Is Parsons still in the house?" Bobby asked.

Sipowicz nodded. "First-floor holding cell. Probably get transferred to the House of D, tomorrow." His lip curled into a sneer. "If I'd had another five minutes with that maggot, I'da got the name of his partner and we'd had the whole pretty package."

"He lawyered up with James Sinclair, I hear."

"Yeah. Sinclair's probably tipped the partner off by now; he's probably in the process of takin' a powder. You know, this guy, this other button guy, him and Parsons, they're doin' the forbidden dance of love."

"No kidding," Bobby said. "So that's why he won't give his partner up."

"Yeah. They're star-crossed. They're just not makin' hit men like they used to." Sipowicz rolled his eyes, shook his head, grunted a laugh. "Medavoy said when Parsons demanded his phone call, he wanted to make it on his *cell* phone."

Bobby's smile had barely formed before it turned into a frown, a thoughtful one. "Parsons had a cell phone on him?"

"Yeah, that's what Medavoy, Russell said."

Bobby sat forward, urgency in his voice. "Is it here?"

"Is what where?"

"The cell phone. I mean, if Parsons is still in the house, they must've checked his valuables downstairs."

"Yeah, so?"

"When Diane and Greg made the collar, Parsons was alone, right?"

"If he'd had his pal with him," Sipowicz said, "we wouldn't be havin' this conversation."

"And the information we had about Parsons said he was into gourmet dining, the finer things . . . but that the partner was a ghost, nobody has anything on him."

"You can hit the 'total' button anytime, pal, 'cause this ain't addin' up for me."

Bobby began to smile. "Don't you see? This dining out, this gourmet thing, it's not a mutual interest. Parsons goes out, his partner stays home. So, who is Parsons talkin' to on his cell phone?"

Sipowicz shrugged. "He could be keepin' in touch with his employer."

"Who right now is in the hospital with a stroke."

"Well, he sure ain't callin' the wife and kids back home."

"No. But he might be checking in with his significant-other-slash-business partner."

Now Sipowicz got it. "Let's reach out and touch some hump."

In the stairwell, as they both practically ran down the steps, Sipowicz said, "Let's not spread this news around."

"Hey, it's just a notion."

"I mean, if we get somethin', I mean, hell—we don't even have a name on this guy."

"We should check it out ourselves before bothering Loo with it."

"My thinking exactly. It's about shift change time, why trouble Night Tour with what's probably a wild goose chase?"

The desk sergeant got them the prisoner's effects, which were in a small wire basket: a billfold, some Marlboros, and the cellular phone. The two detectives huddled over by the wire-mesh wall of the stairwell. Bobby took a look at the billfold.

"They strip the credit cards and identification from this?" he asked Sipowicz.

"No. Russell said there was nothin' but cash in it. Couple hundred . . . and a picture of the two love-birds in the Bahamas or somethin'." Sipowicz hit the PWR button on cell phone, and its little window lit up with the message ON.

Sipowicz hit Redial.

After three rings, he heard a woman's voice musically intone, "Hotel Saville, good evening—how may I direct your call?"

Sipowicz's thumb touched End.

"This is too good," Sipowicz said.

"What?"

"He's at the Saville. That's where the feds kept Giardella. Alfonse even got himself whacked there."

"Small world."

"Real small. I got connections there."

Bobby winced in amused disbelief. "You got connections at the Saville? Isn't the Upper East Side a little off your beat, Andy?"

"I know the head chef, there. Frank Cannady. Got him outta trouble when he tried to serve up some sausage tartare, out on the stroll one night."

Sipowicz had arranged for a soliciting charge against the chef to go away in return for serving Alfonse Giardella some room service lasagna laced with dog shit.

"Parsons is such a gourmet," Sipowicz said, "maybe I should arrange for the chef to whip up some of that beef di merde for him, too."

"Think Cannady could get us a passkey?" Bobby wondered.

Sipowicz pushed Redial again. "Let's see if he's workin' tonight."

Across from the Barbizon School on 63rd at Lexington Avenue, the elegantly remodeled older hotel that was the Saville—marble-floored lobby with rosewood pillars, Chippendale furnishings, and more flower arrangements than a funeral home—certainly fit Leonard Parsons' profile for the finer things.

This time of night, the front desk wasn't very busy; two attractive young women in red blazers and white silk blouses—a black girl with an island lilt to her voice and a name tag that said SINDRA, and a lanky green-eyed brunette with a name tag reading JESSICA—gave the detectives their full attention.

"That is Mr. Parker," Sindra said, pointing to the mug shot of Parsons, though shaking her head at the police sketch of his hawk-faced partner. "But I don't recognize the man in the drawing."

"I'm afraid I don't recognize either gentleman," Jessica said.

Bobby asked Sindra, "You've spoken to Mr. Parker?"

"Yes," Sindra said. "I didn't check him in originally, but he stopped by the desk to extend his stay."

Bobby glanced at Sipowicz, then back at Sindra. "When was that?"

"I believe . . . late Sunday night. They were due to check out the next morning, and Mr. Parker paid for an extra week."

The pair had changed their plans, after the bungled

job at the Sipowicz apartment—and Sipowicz gashing that skinny hawk-faced prick.

Sipowicz said, "What do you mean, 'they'? You said you only recognized Parker, here—"

"Well, as I said, I didn't check him in. He's staying with . . . let me pull this up on the computer." She did. "Yes, here it is. Mr. Parker, Leonard Parker, is sharing a suite with his brother, Ronald."

"Ronald," Sipowicz said, as if tasting the word and not liking it. Still, it was nice finally having a name for the son of a bitch.

Smiling helpfully, Jessica asked, "Would you like me to call up there, and see if either gentleman is in? It is a little late, but—"

Sipowicz held up the mug shot. "This was not taken in one of them little booths, ladies, where you put quarters in and make like a monkey."

That alarmed the two young women, and Bobby tossed Sipowicz a mildly irritated glance.

"Sindra, Jessica," Bobby said, with an ingratiating, calming smile, "these two guests of yours are just people we want to talk to. Part of a routine, preliminary investigation. We don't have warrants—we're just going to knock on the door and, if either gentleman is in, ask a few questions."

Jessica, somewhat placated but with her green eyes still narrowed with concern, said, "Do I need to contact hotel security?"

"Why not?" Sipowicz said.

Bobby nodded. "Even though this is a routine matter, we would like to coordinate with your security."

Sindra picked up the phone and got on that.

Leaning against the counter, Sipowicz said, "Oh, uh, Jessica?"

"Yes?"

"Friend of mine who works here—did he leave an envelope with you, for an Andy Sipowicz? Just a few minutes before we got here . . . he was on his way home?"

"Oh, *you're* Chef Cannady's friend!"

"Yeah. I'm what you call a culinary consultant of his."

She went over to the counter under the mail slots and found an envelope, which she handed him; he slipped it in his side jacket pocket.

The two detectives waited for the security man, over by one of the rosewood pillars. Sipowicz opened the envelope and showed Bobby the key-card.

"That may not do us any good," Bobby said, slipping a stick of gum in his mouth. "The rooms have their own dead bolts, you know. Passkey won't get you past that."

"Then we knock on the door, and take our chances. But if Ronald is waitin' for his honeybun to come home, after an evening out, makin' like Duncan Hines—then the dead bolt maybe ain't thrown. Or the chain, either."

"You're an optimist, Andy."

"Yeah. Polly friggin' Anna."

The security man was a bulky, fiftyish ex-cop named Jacobs who knew Sipowicz a little, from the job. He didn't look as good in the red blazer as the girls behind the front desk had.

"Jake," Sipowicz said, "we got a suspect we're

gonna try to talk to, up in Suite 7114. We're not here to make an arrest, and we don't have a warrant. But I'm not gonna dick you around, Jake—the guy is no angel. He could be packin'."

Jacobs nodded thoughtfully and said, "That suite's at the end of the hall. No rooms on either side."

"There's a break," Sipowicz said.

Bobby said, "Then if you could just stay by the elevator, and hold any people there, who happen along, till we give you the all-clear . . ."

"No problem."

The three men got off the wood-paneled elevator onto the eighth floor, the security man staying behind, walkie-talkie in hand. Rounding the corner from the elevators, they passed a gilt-framed watercolor of fresh-cut flowers below which sat, redundantly, a vase of similar real flowers; near every hotel-room door was a mock gaslight, glowing goldenly. Bathed in this soothing ambiance, Sipowicz—followed by Simone, chewing his gum nervously—moved down the high-ceilinged cream-colored hallway, unbuttoning their jackets as they walked, the plush beige carpeting hiding their footsteps.

At the end of the hall, in a recession that served as a sort of entryway, was the door to Suite 7114. Sipowicz glanced behind him, past Bobby: no one was in sight, no guests, and the security man was around the corner at the elevators. Sipowicz withdrew his .38 and, with one last what-the-hell, over-the-shoulder smirk at Bobby (whose automatic was also in hand), he tried the pass-key card Chef Cannady had provided him. The little green light above the knob flickered on.

Sipowicz tried the door.

It opened.

Sipowicz stepped inside—.38 first—and more plush carpet awaited to conceal his footsteps as he entered the outer room of the suite—sitting area, television, wet bar. A reading lamp beside a peach-colored sofa was the only light source.

Both men were inside, now, guns in hand, Bobby gripping his two-handed; they were the only people in this room. A small bathroom, stool and sink only, was empty. They moved quietly across the outer room toward the open door to the bedroom, where the lights were off, and could see a man in the king-size bed, apparently asleep.

Enough light from the other room filtered in to make it obvious that this was their man, sleeping on his back, under a sheet, like a DOA on a stretcher, skinny, hawk-faced, mid-thirties, his skin a ghostly white, an arm outstretched to reveal a bandaged area, from where Sipowicz slashed him with a shard of fish-tank glass.

Sipowicz stepped inside the room, moved quickly but quietly, with the .38 extended, until he was at the man's bedside, then nodded at Bobby, who hit the light.

As illumination flooded the room, Ronald opened his eyes, squinting up at Sipowicz, saying, "Leonard?"

"No, it's your wake-up call, dickhead," Sipowicz said, and let him look down the nose of the .38, the way the bastard had let Andy look down the barrel of that automatic back in the apartment.

Ronald sat up, a bony, bare-chested apparition, the snakelike eyes fixing themselves on Sipowicz.

"What is this about?" he said, in a mellow, surprisingly cultured voice. Maybe Ronald liked the finer things, too. "Who are you? What are you doing, invading my suite?"

Sipowicz grabbed him by the throat. "Maybe we're a couple hit men here to ice you and the missus."

"Andy," Bobby cautioned.

"Guy tries to kill me," Sipowicz said, "it's common courtesy to remember my goddamn face."

Sipowicz released the guy's throat.

"Police," Bobby said, finally, holding up his badge with one hand, his gun still in the other, and quickly rattled off the Miranda warning. As he did this, Bobby also checked the bathroom off the bedroom, finding it empty. Then he re-assumed his position just inside the doorway.

"This is actionable," Ronald said indignantly, a hand on his neck where Sipowicz had grabbed.

"We already picked up your soul mate," Sipowicz said, keeping the .38 trained on the bare-chested man. "He rolled over on you."

Ronald glowered at Sipowicz. "You're lying."

And of course it was a lie, but at least Sipowicz had finally gotten Ronald to drop the innocent act.

Sipowicz raised his eyebrows, smiled. "Then how d'we find you, Ronald? Leonard also rolled over on Mrs. Giardella . . ."

Hearing that name from Sipowicz made the tiny snake eyes go surprisingly wide.

". . . which may be frowned upon in some circles—the type circles that give disloyal employees goin' away parties in the trunks of cars."

The hawkish features wore dismay openly, now. Still, it wasn't mob retaliation that bothered Ronald; his concern was more personal.

He said, "Leonard would never betray me. . . ."

Sipowicz chuckled. "Tryin' to convince us, or yourself, Ronald?"

Bobby said, "Time to go, Ronald."

Ronald flipped the sheet aside and got off the bed; he was jaybird naked. He didn't have much hair on his body, which made him seem even more naked. Skinny though he was, he did have muscles on him; a wiry strength was apparent. So was a tattoo of a broken heart, on his left arm.

"Get Mapplethorpe here some clothes," Sipowicz said disgustedly.

"They're in the other room," Ronald said. He had his hands on his hips like Superman—naked and unashamed. "Just toss me my robe, and I'll go out there and show you."

"Give him his freakin' robe," Sipowicz said, sick of looking at him.

The wine-colored plush terrycloth robe lay folded neatly over the arm of a chair near Bobby.

Bobby tossed the robe to Ronald, who caught it and in one continuous fluid motion, tossed it at and onto Sipowicz, getting Andy and his .38 caught up in it, covered in it, tangled in the robe, even as the naked man, putting himself between Bobby and Sipowicz, charged Bobby, who hesitated to shoot with Andy so close to the line of fire, and in that brief hesitation, the naked man tackled Bobby, taking him down, sending Bobby's gun flying back through the doorway, bouncing onto the plush carpet in the adjacent room, well out of reach.

By the time Sipowicz got the goddamn robe off him, Ronald was scrambling across the fallen Bobby like a big pink spider, and diving for Bobby's gun on the carpet out there. Sipowicz couldn't get a shot at him through that doorway, not with the dazed Bobby, who was getting on his feet, in the way.

"Bobby, get down!"

Bobby did.

And there Ronald was, a naked man with a gun in his hands, standing out in the other room, framed in the doorway, just behind where Bobby had been standing, the gun pointed at where Bobby had been.

The bullet went in one of the small snake eyes, and life went out of the other. Blood and brains spattered a framed watercolor of flowers over the sofa, turning it into a modern art piece. All motor reflexes had ended with that head shot, and Bobby's gun fell softly to the carpet from limp fingers, and then so did dead naked bony Ronald, depositing himself in a tangle of limbs that looked like a weird yoga position.

"Christ," Bobby said.

"I hope that'll do in lieu of an apology," Sipowicz said, .38 still in hand.

Bobby looked down at Ronald with wide eyes and sighed, "*Oh* yeah."

"You okay, buddy?"

"I swallowed my gum."

Putting the revolver away, Sipowicz quickly stepped out into the hall—Jacobs was running toward him, frantically calling into his walkie-talkie for support from his staff.

"I'll call this in," Sipowicz said, holding up a hand like a cop stopping traffic, barring Jacobs's entry to the hotel suite. "You just get things under control on the hotel end."

"What the hell happened in there?"

Sipowicz shrugged elaborately. "This guy let us in and was actin' real civilized, Jake, then all of sudden pulls down on us. No choice."

Jacobs swallowed thickly. "Shit. Another shooting in the hotel. We're gonna get a bad reputation."

"Two crooks been shot here, Jake. It's not like snipers are pickin' off Rotarians or the plumbers' convention."

Sipowicz slipped back into the hotel room. Closed the door. Flipped the dead bolt.

Bobby was seated in a chair as far away from the dead man as possible; he looked shellshocked. But Sipowicz knew there was no time for that.

"We gotta act fast," he told Bobby. "I'll get him in his robe—he wouldn'ta answered the door with his personality hangin' out like that."

"Okay." Bobby got to his feet, nodding. "Okay."

"And see if you can find a gun in his suitcase or

something. We want him armed, but not with *your* piece."

Bobby's eyes were circles; his mouth, too. "Yeah. Yeah."

"You hangin' in, Bobby?"

"I think so."

A Browning nine millimeter turned up in the nightstand drawer. Sipowicz placed the gun near the right hand of Ronald, who was looking spiffy in his wine-color robe.

Bobby still had a dazed look. "Can we pull this off, Andy?"

"It's our word against his, partner," Sipowicz said, getting to his feet, "and he's dead."

SEVENTEEN

By the time Bobby Simone and Andy Sipowicz got back to the stationhouse, dawn was a memory and they were, technically at least, late for work. Sgt. Agostini was on the front desk and Andy handed in the keys to the unmarked, signed the clipboard, and asked the Sarge if Leonard Parsons had been transferred to the borough House of Detention yet.

"Naw," the sarge said, pointing across the way. "He's still in a holding cell."

Andy nodded, twitched a non-smile, and said, "Think I'll wish him a cheery good morning."

Simone, walking along with Andy, asked quietly, "You think this is a good idea?"

His partner smirked. "I would say prudent kinda went outta the window, a while back."

Parsons was sitting on his cot, eating his breakfast from a plastic tray. Dressed in black as he was, only his white, dark-mustached face, with its eerie resemblance to Andy's, and his equally pale hands, stood out in the dim light, and even they wore the vertical shadows of the cell bars.

"How's our cuisine shape up, Leonard?" Sipowicz asked.

Parsons gave Andy a sneer worthy of Andy himself. "It's not the Four Seasons."

"Ain't the Saville, either."

That got the hired killer's attention. He placed the half-eaten tray of eggs, sausage, and potatoes to one side of him, got up and came over to the bars, facing Andy.

"How'd you come up with that, fatso?"

Andy glanced at Simone, amused. " 'Fatso.' That's quite a cutting insult, coming from a lardass like you. I'm gonna have to check in with my analyst, to handle that one."

"Where's Ronald?"

"Ronald?" Sipowicz frowned in comic confusion. "Who would that be? Oh, now it comes to me. Ronald would be your dead partner. Who I shot in the head, oh, what, Bobby? Three hours ago? Give or take a few minutes."

The moon face turned from pale to a ghastly, ghostly white. He lurched for Sipowicz, who merely stepped back a step, and his thick hands reached through the bars in that hopeless, grasping manner that so many prisoners' hands have assumed through the ages.

"You bastard . . . you heartless bastard . . ."

And Leonard Parsons, hired killer, withdrew his arms from between the bars, stumbled over to the cot, and collapsed, knocking the food tray clatteringly to the cement.

And he began to weep.

"Hurts to lose a loved one, don't it, Leonard?" Sipowicz grunted a mirthless laugh. "Never occurred to you, when you went into the business of whacking out people, the trail of human misery you was leavin' behind . . . mothers, fathers, husbands, wives, kids, cryin' their eyes out over what you done. For money."

"I'll find you . . . I'll fucking kill you. . . ."

"Take a number. By the way, you may want to reconsider your choice of counsel. James Sinclair has already shared your rollin' over on Mrs. G. with his pals at the Sicilian Chamber of Commerce."

Parsons looked up, his tear-streaked face now alive with alarm.

"In other words, Leonard, despite your predicament, you got options. One, some goombah gets you with a shiv, in the big house, or, two—should that immunity thing hold up—you get to have a building put up in your honor by goin' to sleep in its foundation."

Parsons covered his mouth, his hand trembling; his voice did the same, oozing through his splayed fingers: "You're a monster . . . you're inhuman. You . . . you'll burn in hell, you sadistic bastard. . . ."

Sipowicz waved that off. "Aw, I don't think so. Oh, I may do a century or two in purgatory. But meanwhile, Leonard, you'll be spendin' eternity sweepin' up in the Boilin' Lava Room."

Andy swaggered out of there, and Simone followed him out. As they were going up the stairs to the squadroom, Andy did a Rodney Dangerfield, loosening his collar, saying, "Can you picture that sleazeball? Does he think the people he hits don't have friggin' relatives who care about 'em?"

"Alfonse Giardella did," Simone reminded him.

Andy didn't have a reply to that one.

In Room 202, Day Shift had begun, Donna seated at her desk, wearing a red sweater with spangles that shouldn't have been legal at this time of morning; Greg and James were also at their posts, a little bleary-eyed but none the worse for wear, Lesniak, too.

And, of course, Fancy, at his desk behind the glass-and-wood wall of his office, on the phone, having an animated conversation with somebody, or as animated a conversation as Fancy was capable of having. Only Diane was missing in action.

Simone pushed through the gate into the bullpen, a twitchy Andy behind him, eyes deep in their dark sockets, a sweep of his palm brushing back the memory of hair. Greg and James scurried over.

"We been hearin' some pretty wild stuff," James said, with an expression that seemed poised between smile and frown, ready to go either way.

"What you hear is true," Andy said. "My shlong really is that big."

Greg said, "You got the other guy? Parsons' roommate?"

Andy nodded, touched his forehead with a fingertip. "I converted him to Buddhism. He's wearin' a dot right here."

Through the window of his office, Fancy was looking at them with vague disgust; he was still talking on the phone, however—they had not yet been summoned.

"Three, four hours," Simone said to Greg and James, sighing, shaking his head, "dancin' with 15th Precinct cops, Homicide squad, an inspector from downtown. . . ."

"Doesn't sound like f-fun," Greg admitted.

"Much as I'd like to chat, I got a WDR to write up," Andy said, heading to his desk. "Kinda makes me wish I took that night school class in creative writing."

"I better start typing myself," Simone said wearily.

Before he began the report, Andy made a phone call, or tried to. Hanging up, he said, "Wonder where the hell Sylvia is."

Simone looked up from his typewriter. "Where you tryin' her, at home?"

"Yeah. She wasn't goin' in today."

Andy had spoken to Sylvia, at length, on the phone, from the hotel. So she was up to speed, at least on the official story, which was that Andy and Simone had been admitted to the hotel room of Ronald Parker, that Andy—recognizing Parker as one of the assailants who broke into his apartment—had placed him under arrest, Mirandizing him, Parker seeming cooperative, and when Andy had been searching the bedroom, with Bobby and the perp in the outer room, the perp had taken advantage of Bobby turning away to somehow come up with a gun, and Andy had been forced to shoot him, from the bedroom, through the doorway.

Andy had just finished typing up the Weapons

Discharge Report when Fancy stepped from his office and gave both Simone and Andy a look that was all it took to summon them into his chamber.

Soon Andy and Simone were seated before the lieutenant's desk while he read Andy's WDR and Simone's statement.

"Neither one of you were working this case," Fancy said.

"We was just chasin' a wild lead, Loo," Sipowicz said. "I mean, Bobby's makin' like Sherlock Holmes with this redial cell-phone notion, and I'm just Doctor What's-It goin' along for the ride."

"We didn't have any idea it would really pan out, Loo," Simone said.

"Don't insult my intelligence," Fancy said. He sighed. "On a certain level, this was a good piece of police work."

"Thanks," Sipowicz said.

"Don't take that as a compliment. I won't put up with this kind of thing, from my squad. If either of you engage in this kind of Dodge City campaign again, you'll be working radio dispatch in Siberia. . . . Am I clear?"

"Clear," Andy said.

"Clear," Simone said.

"Now go home, and don't answer the phone," Fancy said, not looking at either of them. "God knows what the media's gonna do with this."

"I can handle the media," Sipowicz said, standing.

"Don't even try," Fancy said. "I don't want one of your choice remarks showing up anywhere. And let's pray I.A.B. doesn't get involved."

Andy frowned. "Really think this is a Rat Squad matter?"

"I think Bobby's okay, though the question may be raised as to why a perp this dangerous wasn't handcuffed upon his arrest. *You* were out of policy, Andy. I warned you. At the very least look for a rip."

"A little loss in pay ain't gonna kill me."

"Let's hope that's all that comes of it."

Andy paused at the door and asked, "Loo . . . you think Inspector Bass will make this a good shooting?"

Fancy sighed. "Yeah. I already talked to him. He's gonna sign off on it. That much you got going for you. Get some rest, then get your asses over to Le-Frak City for the mandatory counseling."

Relief flooded Andy's face. "Thank you, Loo."

Fancy wore a stonier mask than usual, however, and his eyes burned. "Don't make me do any more favors for you, Andy. That bank account's just about played out."

"Okay, boss."

Simone and Andy moved back toward their desks.

"What did I tell you?" Andy said. "The boss is so proud of us, we get the day off."

"Let's try not to make him that proud again," Simone said, then nodded over toward the entry area. "Look, there . . ."

Diane was trudging into the squadroom, with Sylvia following, briefcase in hand; both women looked gaunt, weary.

Andy and Simone knew at once something was wrong, and moved through the bullpen gate and stood by the catching bench, opposite Donna's desk, and faced them.

"I thought you were goin' home," Andy said to his wife.

"We got called over to Central Park West," she said, nodding in Diane's direction. Sylvia's eyes had that bright, glazed look they got when something terrible had happened. "It was a case affecting both of us. . . ."

"What?" Simone asked.

Andy's expression asked the same question.

Diane sighed; it seemed to come up from her shoes. "Laura Wynn has just been arrested for the murder of her father."

Simone and Andy exchanged puzzled looks.

"You mean, 'mother,' " Simone said to Diane.

"No." Diane shook her head, as if she couldn't believe it herself. "She slashed her father to death last night, with a broken bourbon bottle. . . . Her aunt found them, this morning. Blood everywhere . . ."

"Jesus," Simone said.

"Christ," Andy said.

"They're holding her at Bellevue for psychiatric observation," Diane said.

Simone, exhausted from the longest night of his life, felt dizzy, suddenly; he sat, almost collapsed, on the catching bench, holding his head in his hands.

"She opened in that play, this weekend," he said hollowly.

Andy sat next to his partner. "Maybe the understudy'll go on and there'll be a happy ending."

Nobody said anything for a while. Phones rang,

typewriters clacked, and outside a police siren whined. Then Sylvia Costas gathered up her husband and took him home.

And Diane Russell sat next to Bobby Simone, not touching him, not saying anything, just there for him.

Max Allan Collins has earned an unprecedented seven Private Eye Writers of America "Shamus" nominations for his "Nathan Heller" historical thrillers, winning twice (*True Detective*, 1983, and *Stolen Away*, 1991). The latest Heller novel is *Damned in Paradise* (1996).

A Mystery Writers of America "Edgar" nominee in both fiction and nonfiction categories, Collins has been hailed as "the Renaissance man of mystery fiction." His credits include four suspense-novel series, film criticism, short fiction, songwriting, trading-card sets, graphic novels, and occasional movie tie-in novels, including such best-sellers as *In the Line of Fire*, *Maverick*, and *Waterworld*.

He scripted the internationally syndicated comic strip "Dick Tracy" from 1977–1993, is co-creator of the comic-book feature *Ms. Tree*, and has written both the *Batman* comic book and newspaper strip. His science-fiction comic-book featured *Mike Danger* (co-created with Mickey Spillane), is in development as a major motion picture by Miramax.

Working as an independent filmmaker in his native

Iowa, he wrote, directed, and executive-produced *Mommy*, a suspense telefilm starring Patty McCormack and Jason Miller, which aired on Lifetime in 1996; he performed the same duties for a sequel, *Mommy 2: Mommy's Day* (1997). He is also the screenwriter of *The Expert*, a 1995 HBO World Premiere film.

Collins lives in Muscatine, Iowa, with his wife, writer Barbara Collins, and their teenage son, Nathan.

SIGNET **ONYX**

SHOCKING TRUE-CRIME

☐ **DONNIE BRASCO My Undercover Life In the Mafia A True Story by FBI Agent Joseph D. Pistone with Richard Woodley. The National Best-seller!** Posing as jewel thief "Donnie Brasco," Joseph D. Pistone carried out the most audacious sting operation ever. Now his unforgettable eyewitness account brings to pulsing life the entire world of wiseguys and draws a chilling picture of what the Mafia is, does, and means in America today. **"Courageous and extraordinary"**—*New York Times Book Review* (192575—$6.99)

☐ **KILLING SEASON The Unsolved Case of New England's Deadliest Serial Killer by Carlton Smith.** With in-depth research and eye-opening new testimony, this enthralling true-crime masterpiece is the story of the horrifying victimization of women, their vicious murders, and shocking official impotence. (405463—$5.99)

☐ **CHAIN OF EVIDENCE A True Story of Law Enforcement and One Woman's Bravery by Michael Detroit.** This thrilling, true account of a woman undercover police officer who infiltrated the Hell's Angels in Orange County, California, reveals as never before the dangerous risks and the exciting triumph of a law enforcement operation over a far-reaching crime network. (404629—$5.99)

☐ **DEADLY THRILLS The True Story of Chicago's Most Shocking Killer by Jaye Slade Fletcher. With 8 pages of photos.** Here is the startling true account of a "boy-next-door" electrician whose twisted desires produced unspeakable havoc in the Chicago area. This incredible but all-too-real journey will take you into the heart of Robin Gecht, a monstrously evil man who ritually multilated his victims and subjected their bodies to shocking acts of sexual violation. (406257—$5.99)

*Prices slightly higher in Canada